Cassia's Calling

Rachel Blanchard

1

Thunderous knocking on the heavy oak door was jarring, but not uncommon. Cassia leapt from her straw mattress and unlatched the door.

It was Benaniah, the village baker and a repeat customer. Thankfully not sporting any blood. He was, however, wincing and holding his right ear. Cassia's eye focus grew hazy as she mentally scanned for the injury with a physician's precision. Without a touch, without a word, she could sense that his jaw muscle was tighter than a sailor's knot.

She shook her head. Ben was surely worrying about the lack of rainfall again. It took all of her patience not to relax the muscle right then, but she had to keep up pretenses of being a traditional healer.

"Mother," she called, more than a little alarmed that her mother hadn't already awoken on the straw tick she shared with Cassia. So exhausted from bringing in the wheat harvest? Though Aline wouldn't admit how many summers she'd seen, she was showing signs of age.

Her mother's eyes shot open, revealing the eerie silver that often had them labeled as cursed, though that couldn't be farther from the truth. Ben, however, was used to the sight.

"I'm sorry, I know it's early," he said. "I couldn't get to sleep and was hoping you'd have more of that chamomile oil. My wife bought me a vial at market, but it just doesn't seem to work as well as yours."

After a half-dozen years of isolation in the forest, Cassia knew better than to share a wary look with her adoptive mother.

"We have an excellent supplier over in Soliea. As usual, you've come to the right place," Aline lied smoothly. "I'll prepare you a draught at once." She plucked a glass bottle out of their cabinet, poured a few drops of its contents into a wooden cup, and let Ben drink. "It's extremely potent. You should feel the effects in a few moments."

Cassia closed her eyes and refocused on the tensed jaw muscle. Incrementally, she loosened each fiber.

"Potent stuff," Ben repeated. He studied the pair before shaking his head clear.

That was why Aline allowed Cassia to heal Ben. He might have had a keen eye, but he had a closed mouth, and as long as his earaches were cured, he didn't ask questions.

"I brought these for you." Ben held up a sack of fresh bread loaves.

"Thank you, kindly." Cassia took the load. "We hope you have a pleasant morning. Please tell your wife hello for us."

"I surely will." Ben nodded, polite as ever. That was another good thing about Ben. Like all of their handful of trusted clients, he sensed enough otherworldliness in the air not to hang around.

As the door closed, Aline sunk back into the mattress.

"It's fine, Mother. It's not like it's King Peter knocking at the door," Cassia joked. Aline did not smile in return.

"Once you've lived as long as I have, you'll understand why we have to keep our distance."

They'd likely receive no visitors at all, if they could afford to live off the forest's bounty alone. But times were hard for tax-paying citizens, who'd foraged further and further inland until there was little left, even for two lone women, to glean. So, Cassia and Aline had filled in the gaps by beginning trade with a few discreet neighbors. "Was the king always this bad?" Cassia asked.

Aline hated talking about her old life in the palace, but Cassia was desperate to reopen the subject. After all, how was she supposed to keep herself safe from a danger she didn't fully understand? That's what she told her mother, at least. The truth was, Cassia was wildly curious about the outside world, the one she only experienced in novels.

Aline sighed as she returned the chamomile oil to the cabinet. "I knew the king when he was just a boy. And he wasn't always selfish and greedy. A tad aloof, perhaps, which is why he allows himself to be manipulated by that snake of a man, Radomir."

She shuddered. "But don't you pity him. We all have choices as to who we are going to be. For a man of influence like Peter, the choice to be good matters tenfold. Instead, he sticks his head in the sand and lets his people starve. Turns a blind eye when his stewards exact taxes through lying and blood. Trust me. I thank the Maker every day that I am far away from Lynebrook."

Cassia was mystified as to how Aline still believed in a Maker, when she was sent running for her life six years ago, simply for being too late to save Peter's betrothed. Now she was fated to live as a hermit the rest of her life. It seemed a gross injustice to Cassia, but there was no use arguing about that, either.

Aline always said that finding sixteen-year-old Cassia bleeding out after a robber's attack, with her family dead all around her, was the Maker's way of making good out of the evil Peter had done by chasing Aline out of the royal city.

Aline had sacrificed her healing powers to save Cassia's life, transferring the gift to her at the price of Cassia's earlier memories. They were all each other had, and Cassia feared, the way Aline's health had been, that they may not have each other much longer. "But isn't there anything to be done? You lived at the royal court."

"Yes, and I'd prefer not to speak any more on the subject. We will stay here and keep our gifts unnoticed from prying eyes, so that we may continue to help those around us."

It made sense, but somehow, performing healings at one hundredth of her true healing ability did not feel significant to Cassia.

Aline, as usual, seemed to read Cassia's mind, and ran a steadying hand down her daughter's silky blond locks, which had escaped from her long braid thanks to the unexpected interruption. "Always trying to save the world. You're doing enough, young one. Have patience."

Cassia nodded and turned to busy her hands with Ben's dirty cup so she'd feel like less of a liar.

"Cassia, dear, we're running short on rue. Can you go to the patch today and fetch some?"

Cassia held in a groan. It was so frustrating to go through so much effort for mere stage props. The rue patch was a whole morning's walk away. "I'll go now, while it's still cool outside."

She cracked open one of the cottage's shutters. Mist rose from the ground like this really was an enchanted place. But Aline attributed her gift to the Maker. To a source of magic beyond time and place. And it was true, there were no incantations needed.

Healing was inside of Cassia, a part of her, and reaching out and sensing others came as naturally as the breath in her own lungs, though the effort of healing took a toll. She was still human, after all. At least, that's what Aline insisted.

Cassia wrapped a shawl around herself and looped a basket in the crook of her arm.

Although at times Cassia delayed working outside, once her legs were moving, her mind appreciated the productive exercise. At least a nature walk freed her from the monotony of the cottage.

Aline frequently accused her of being a dreamer, pretending as if she regretted giving her the education of a noblewoman, but Cassia could see how she held affection and pride behind her stern expression.

Cassia stroked the moss on the oak trunks as she passed, and joined the morning sparrow's song with a ditty of her own:

If I were as free as a bird

I'd fly

To the pinnacle of heaven,

the sky!

Cassia laughed at her foolishness. She had her health and a mother who loved her more than life. She oughtn't complain or wish for more.

As she approached the clearing where the rue grew, Cassia froze. Male voices lifted in bickering, in panic. Unconsciously, Cassia's mind honed in on the source of the stress. A gash, a few inches deep, on a man's arm.

Cassia clutched at the bark of the nearest tree, attempting to ground herself back in reality as Aline had taught her. But the man's pain kept pulling her back. He could die of blood loss or infection.

Maybe if she didn't allow herself to be seen...there was no way she could attempt to heal a wound with herbs the way she had feigned curing an earache. Could she really leave him to die?

Another cry, and Cassia could help it no longer. She slunk deeper into the shadows of the forest and closed her eyes, picturing each fiber of the muscle stitching back together. She opened her eyes and breathed deeply, relieved, as she knew the work had been done. But the men had grown eerily quiet.

She had to go. She'd collect the rue another day, if Aline would even think it safe to return. Cassia hastened back the way she'd come, but her limbs felt sluggish. She should have considered what the more taxing repair would do to her energy supply.

She tried breathing in the cool air, feeling the rising sun heat her face, but her pace grew slower as her panic increased. It wasn't safe to stop and slumber with these men nearby. Who were they? Loggers? Bandits? Soldiers?

Her next step was unsteady until her consciousness whooshed into nothingness.

2

"I've heard whispers of a witch around these parts," Mack grumbled.

Fearless as ever, he had been the one to hoist the young woman over his shoulder and carry her back to camp. Guy couldn't stop running his fingers over his forearm, where a nasty gash, courtesy of Mack's wicked axe, was gone—only a crust of dried blood remained to convince Guy it hadn't been all in his head.

"How do you know she's a witch?" Guy asked.

"They say her hair is as pale as the midsummer moon. All the better to entice men with her beauty, into their deaths." His gravelly tone grew to a storyteller's hush, and Guy wished he would just hush altogether.

"She didn't lead me to my death. She saved me."

"This time," Mack said, eyebrows raised suggestively.

"What do you think, Stephen?" Guy turned to his former neighbor, who'd connected Guy with Mack's family over their common frustration with Peter's reign.

The older man among their company was slower to speak than Mack, who was often the leader in both size and bluster. However, Guy valued Stephen's quiet wisdom.

Stephen stroked his gray mustache. "Let's see what she says when she wakes."

"Maybe she can help us!" Roland jogged up to his father and looked at the prone woman with fairy dust in his eyes.

"Don't you breathe a word of the plan to this wench, boy. We don't know hide nor hair about her. She could strike us down and then go running straight to the palace for a reward."

When the camp came into view, Guy said, "You can lay her in my tent."

Mack wasn't a cruel or immoral man, but he was a man with much to protect, and much to lose. Guy didn't know if he always saw the most clearly when it came to interferences from "the plan."

Besides, a pang of pity squeezed at Guy's heart at the sight of the woman's head nodding back and forth against Mack's shoulder.

She couldn't be more than a few years over twenty, barely younger than him. She'd be terrified to wake up among a group of rabble-rousers such as themselves.

Mack lay the woman upon Guy's straw tick and Guy dropped the tent curtain closed.

Mack harrumphed. "You stand watch now. She could go sliding out the back and to the authorities, quicker than a hare in a hunt."

"Yes, sir." Guy saluted, dropped down to the grass, and put his back against a tree. He peered back into the tent, just to make sure the maiden still slept. What had made her pass out so suddenly and soundly? "If she is the one who healed my arm, we owe her a great thanks. You nearly maimed me."

"We'll be more careful next time."

Guy's head sunk between his bent knees. "How are we going to kill King Peter if we're nearly killing ourselves in a sparring match? He'll have dozens of guards at the palace."

Mack rehearsed his speech, emphasizing each point with the side of his hand. "We infiltrate the palace in disguise. He won't see us coming. We get close enough. It only takes one strike."

Guy gulped. They'd have to expect that they might be plotting a suicide mission. But he'd just have to pray he'd make it back to free his father from debtor's prison—so they could have a future together.

Delicate fingers whipped the fabric of Guy's tent entrance open. "Well, that's the least intelligent idea I've ever heard."

Mack grappled for his axe. Guy waved him away. "How much did you hear?"

"You have nothing to fear from me. My mother and I have no love for King Peter." She winced, as though regretting the mention of her family.

Mack extended himself to his full, bear-like height. "You can't return to her now."

"Mack." Guy warned. "Will adding kidnapping to our crimes really aid our plot?"

"We can't risk it." He stabbed a finger in the woman's direction. "She's heard too much."

Her face remained smooth. "I won't breathe a word. My mother and I are isolated, and we don't talk to anyone. Your secret couldn't be in safer hands."

"So your mother won't come investigating. And you have secrets of your own, don't you, young one?"

The woman clamped her lips together and folded her arms, though her already pale face blanched. She had such strange, ice-blue eyes, like she truly was an enchantress from a frozen land.

"May we at least know your name?" Guy entreated.

"I'm Cassia. And you are..."

Mack shook his head, but Guy ignored him. "I'm Guy. Just a humble farmer's son, with no father and no grain to harvest, thanks to the king's taxes."

"I'm sorry. I've heard of many in the same situation as you." Her eyes flashed to Mack. "How do you know about me and my mother?"

"We're friends with the baker in town."

"Apparently, Ben isn't as discreet as we thought." Her face crumpled.

"He's a good man, but that is a mighty strange secret to keep. Whispers creep out. Two women, alone in the forest, with unearthly powers."

Cassia bristled. "There's nothing unearthly about what I do. I gain strength from the earth, nearly had my face in it after I made the mistake of healing one of your men."

"I say we let her free," Roland chimed in, grinning like a fool. Guy figured he'd noticed Cassia's expressive, downturned eyes, oval face, and willowy frame, and was hoping to gain sympathy. But he was too young for her. Wasn't he?

Guy ran his hands through his burnt sienna curls. What a time to think about women. Maybe Mack was right. His focus was far off. "Would you consider traveling with us? Your healing abilities could be of much use."

Mack clapped his paws on either side of his bald head. "We don't need any witch's spells! And anyway, she could run away."

Guy shrugged. "I'll keep an eye on her. What else would you suggest?"

Cassia cleared her throat. All four men turned to regard her. "Can you tell me more of this plan? Once you depose the king, who will rule?"

Guy stood, reinvigorated. "The next in line, Cristian, is said to be much more merciful, but overshadowed by the grip of the royal advisor."

"And he'll just listen to all that you say, will he, when he discovers that you've murdered his brother? What's to stop Radomir from seizing the throne himself?"

"We'll be in danger, no doubt, but we hope to sneak away undetected. If the worst happens, we'll regroup."

"If your attack makes it through the palace's defenses due to the 'element of surprise,' which is highly unlikely, do you think they would allow fugitives to infiltrate their guard a second time?"

Guy acknowledged, "The plan has flaws, but we're desperate, Miss. I'll never make enough money to free my father. And, even if he were freed, what kind of life would he live?"

Roland's tone grew solemn. "My sister died from an illness a year back." Mack tensed. "They call it a tragedy, but I know the truth. If she would've had enough food, she would have been able to fight it. Peter has to go, and Radomir and our Lord John with 'im."

"Now you're talking about three murders!"

"Just one," Guy clarified. "I believe once Cristian is in power, he won't put up with Radomir's manipulations. Cristian is always protesting on behalf of the poor against the unjust lords but is largely ignored."

"So Peter is that thick-headed?"

Roland nodded. "Our cousin is a maid in the palace. She said the death of his betrothed broke him. He's more like to deal with the pain through more apathy, and even cruelty, than to open up his heart again."

"The fact is," Mack stepped closer, "you'll be coming with us, whether ya like it or not. And it'd be much simpler if we didn't have to drag you around with your arms tied together."

Just then, a woman with hair so light red it was nearly pink emerged from the tree line, setting down a cloth full of berries. "What in the heavens, Mack? Threatening a poor maiden."

"Gisella," Mack blustered, his forehead wrinkling before he set his face. "This maiden listened in on our plans. We have to take her with us now."

Gisella's face flashed to Cassia's with compassion. She plucked up Cassia's hand. "There, there, dear. They're not as bad as they seem."

Cassia backed away. "What? What happened to the discussion about letting me go?"

Gisella's mouth turned down. "You see, my family's got into some dangerous business. I'm afraid we're all a little on-edge."

Guy asked, "Would it help if we let you tell your mother that you are safe?"

He didn't like the calculating gleam behind Cassia's eyes as she said. "Very well. Let me speak with my mother. I promise to return..."

"I will accompany you, of course."

Cassia huffed. "And I won't be directly involved with this plot of yours?"

"You'd only have to heal us. Hopefully even that won't be necessary. You, Gisella, and Roland—" Roland shouted his standard protest at this " —will be planted far away from the action."

"All right," Cassia said, chin held high as an empress. "Let's go."

3

The trek back to the cottage was surreal. This morning, Cassia's mission had been an annoying chore. This afternoon, Cassia was under threat of sword by a handsome man who, though his weapon was sheathed, she was sure wouldn't hesitate to catch her should she try to escape.

It was no matter. She'd escape him after a time of pretending to be on their side. Though, she had to admit feeling a sick sense of adventure at this departure from her everyday routine.

Aline would know what to do. She'd figure something out for Cassia, as she always did.

"Did you steal your sword?" Cassia asked.

Guy scrubbed at the dark scruff starting to sprout on his jaw. "We took weapons off some fallen soldiers at the Lancily line."

"I can see why you all are on edge. I'm surprised the bailiff hasn't put you in irons by now."

"There are ways, which it sounds like you know, to stay on the fringes. Ben passes us bread. We fish. Move along by the streams."

"Making your way to Lynebrook?"

"Not yet. There's just the slight problem of access to the palace. Still, I'll be wanted soon for being late on my father's payments, so it's best not to stay in one place."

Cassia quickened her pace, leaving Guy to jog to keep up with her. If she needed a reminder of the peril of her situation, that was it.

Perhaps a league before their cottage, the acrid stench of smoke filled Cassia's nostrils. The air became hazy as her stride sped into a sprint.

Flames, hot and hungry, licked at the wood of the only home she'd ever known. And a deep blue Lynebrook flag whipped merrily in the wind, plunged into the soil before the door.

"Mother!" Cassia screamed. The king had found them out. For what? Tax evasion? Such unexpected, public destruction was unheard of, even by Lynebrook's oppressive standards. This statement was targeted. This statement was personal.

Word must have reached Peter about the supernatural healings in the forest. Since he didn't know about Cassia, he'd assumed that this new activity was performed by the woman who'd once failed to save his betrothed. The woman who'd fled six years ago and evaded punishment.

Cassia ran to the cottage, ignoring Guy's shouts behind her. He needn't have worried. The soldiers were long gone. And so was her mother's spirit.

Cassia threw herself to the ground by Aline's bloodstained body, sensing before seeing that there was no breath in the lungs and no pulse of the heart. Still, she threw her healing powers into the corpse, willing the Maker to bring her mother back to life. She pushed once, twice, three, times, before fading into oblivion.

A young man with tousled golden hair stood above Cassia, weeping. "Save her!" he called beyond his shoulder. Then he turned back to Cassia, stroking back her hair. "This is all my fault. I never should have let you fight."

"No," Cassia protested, sure this was untrue, though she had no idea who this boy was. She looked down at her chest, which was getting harder to raise with breath, and was shocked to see an arrow protruding there.

She reached out for the boy before her arm went limp, thudding on the ground.

Cassia drew in a sharp breath and opened her eyes. Night was falling around her. She was still beside her cottage, not in a sunlit battlefield. Guy stood beside her, balancing his weight against their garden shovel, looking at her hesitantly and standing next to a large hole in the ground.

Oh. Cassia closed her eyes. She would prefer to stay in the nightmare.

"Cassia?" Guy coaxed. He inched closer, and she rolled away.

"Cassia, I'm so very sorry."

With arms that felt as rigid as bars of steel, Cassia heaved herself to a sitting position.

Guy hadn't changed Aline's bloody tunic, but he had pulled it straight and folded her arms into a more peaceful posture. He'd brushed her hair back and closed her lifeless eyes.

"Thank you," Cassia sniffled. She brushed her fingers against Aline's cheekbones. "What am I going to do now?"

"Come back with me. Only if you want to. I'll deal with Mack if not, but if you come, I promise you'll be safe. You need something to eat and a place to rest..." he trailed off, likely wondering why it was that Cassia'd passed out this morning and again just now. But there was no reason to act mysterious any longer.

"I want to help you." Cassia didn't want to return with Guy because he was a nice man and because she could help him, should he be injured again. She wanted to hurt the king.

How could Peter's grievance against her mother run so deep that he had hunted her all this way like a fox and murdered her so brutally?

"I'm sorry, there's nothing salvageable in your house." Guy lifted the shovel. "I found this in your garden shed."

"There was nothing of value, anyway. Mother was the only important thing." Cassia leapt to her feet and towards the flower field, desperate to occupy herself. She pulled the stems of a dozen violet blooms to lay in the chilled fingers that had once wiped away Cassia's tears and patted away all anxiety.

"Sleep now, my sweet, selfless mother. I'll do my best to make you proud."

Guy put a gentle hand on her back. "I can do the rest."

Cassia stumbled off to the tree line as Guy scooped her mother up. She didn't want to see him lay her in the earth. How she hated that this was the last time she would ever see her. Cassia picked more violets to adorn the mound of dirt that would conceal her only family for all time.

Only the crickets chattered over the crackle of the campfire. The once boisterous voice of Mack was reduced to a whisper.

"I'm sorry I was so hard on you this morning, lass."

Cassia said nothing. She was glad Guy had explained to the group what had happened upon their return, out of her earshot.

"King Peter's taken from us all." Gisella's voice shook.

"Your daughter," Cassia murmured, recalling their conversation from earlier.

"Aye."

Talking with strangers about someone else was easier than talking about herself. And even in her pain, Cassia was not immune to what Gisella's pain must have been. "What was she like?"

"That child was as wild as a wolf cub, I'll tell you that." Gisella's eyes turned heavenwards. "She was always stringing posies through her hair or following frogs down the banks of the creek. That was the worst part. When she was abed. Roland even brought her pet goose in to pay her a visit."

Roland stalked off toward his tent, and Gisella rose to follow.

"Give him a moment, love," Mack put a gentle hand on his wife's shoulder, his own eyes glistening with tears.

Cassia plucked at the knotted ends of her hair. "My mother called me wild-spirited. I wish I had paid her more heed."

Gisella's voice was soft. "She knew you loved her, I'm right sure of that."

How Cassia wished to believe the woman's assurance. "Can you be sure of that? You didn't know her."

"Mothers have a way of knowing more than they let on, and for soaking up the hundred tiny ways they're told 'I love you.'"

"My mother taught me to play the strings. Perhaps some music would ease your mind?" Guy looked to Cassia.

She nodded, and he disappeared inside his tent. She'd been too exhausted to notice anything before, but sure enough, a fiddle had been inside.

Guy coaxed out a song dripping with sadness and then soaring with hope. It was a tune Cassia recognized. She joined in, her voice unsteady:

Once, I lost my love
> They off and wandered away
> I set my course to seek them
> But nevermore I may

Once, I lost my love
> Caught in the Maker's embrace
> Toil here no more to chase
> When night shines forth as day.

Her vibrato shook on the final note.

Gisella clutched her hands to her chest. "Goodness, Cassia, you have the most lovely voice I've heard. You sound like a fallen star."

"Because I've plummeted down to Earth?"

"Nay, because it seems you should be shining above us. You are gifted in more ways than one. My soprano sounds more like the squeaking of an old cart wheel!"

Mack added, "Or the braying of the mule pulling it."

"You must stop being so honest, dear."

"Sorry," he put his hands out in deference. "I'd best turn in or my wife will do me in before Guy gets another shot while sparring."

"I'll come, too. Maybe I can fall asleep before you wake the forest with your snores."

They walked away arm in arm. At least they had each other to find comfort in. Cassia felt so alone, even amidst the thoughtful gestures of her new acquaintances.

Stephen stood and stretched. "It's too late for my old bones. Rest well. I am sorry for your loss."

"Thank you," Cassia said softly. For someone who could analyze every piece of tissue in the lungs, she was having difficulty drawing breath.

"So," she turned to Guy to distract herself, terrified he would want to go to sleep as well, and leave her with her thoughts. "How do farmers go about weapons training?"

"My grandfather was a disgraced knight. He escaped an arranged marriage to run away with a peasant girl and taught me a few things before he passed."

Guy drew his sword, and Cassia noticed for the first time the fine chiseling on the inky hilt. The blade also featured an inscription: "By the Maker's Strength."

"I didn't take this off a fallen soldier. This, believe it or not, is a family heirloom, carefully hidden from the bailiff's rounds."

"It sounds like revolution runs in the family."

"I wish it didn't have to." Guy sheathed his sword and glared into the fire. "I'd love to free my father, go back home. Live a simple and honest life. But under this regime, it's impossible. And, as scared as it makes me, I have to try."

"How did you lose your mother?" Cassia asked gently.

"She died giving birth to my baby brother. My brother didn't make it, either." Guy looked at Cassia, as if he needed her approval. "Now you see why my father is all I have. He's growing ill, and I won't get him back with Westcombe stealing my profits."

"Does your father know about your plans?"

"No. I didn't want to put him at risk. I just said I loved him, and that I couldn't visit him anymore until I worked hard enough to secure his freedom."

"Not untrue, I suppose. Would he disapprove, if he knew what you were doing?"

"He would. My father is honest to a fault. It should be a benefit, if the kingdom wasn't what it was."

Aline would want Cassia to keep herself safe, to keep herself hidden. Well, Aline wasn't around to keep Cassia bound anymore. All their care had led to devastation, anyway.

What kind of life would Cassia have without her mother's teaching, her daily tasks constructed to keep their minds and bodies active when they couldn't reach out and be a part of their greater community?

A chilling wind whipped through the trees, making Cassia shiver. Guy retrieved the wool blanket from his tent and put it around her shoulders.

"Won't you get cold?" she asked, despite pulling the blanket closer.

He grinned. "I have thick skin."

Cassia shook her head. "You have the heart of a true knight."

Guy lifted one shoulder. "But only half the pedigree."

Cassia took in a deep breath of wood smoke, her muscles finally relaxing. "Thank you for your kindness."

"Real kind, repaying you for saving me by seizing you and holding you prisoner."

"You tried to help me." Cassia replayed the day's events in her mind. Though she didn't understand why her mother had to suffer, she could see a funny sort of providence in the timing of the king's attack.

If Cassia hadn't been delayed by Guy and his men, she would have died, too. "And I don't know what I would have done had I come upon...what we found by myself."

"Aye." Silence hung between them for a moment. "So, do you mind me asking how you do it? How do you heal people?"

Cassia bristled. It was her instinct to conceal everything about her ability. But she had no safe haven anymore. What did she have, besides this band of peasant strangers, bound by a common cause?

"I...feel things. Like my senses extend to you, to any living being if I concentrate enough." She closed her eyes. "I can hear your heartbeat, as far away as you are. Feel each pulse. Every breath." Her eyes snapped open.

"That must be overwhelming."

"Sensing isn't, so much. Most sensations I've learned to block out. It's when I act, to manipulate the body, that drains my energy. I need sleep, quiet, serenity—much like anyone I suppose—just in greater amounts after healing. Yours was the first wound I've healed that was potentially mortal. Usually, I try to stay away from circumstances which could reveal my power."

"Thanks for taking that risk for me."

"It's hard not to, with a life in peril."

Guy appeared to think through all she'd said. "Can you heal illnesses? Fatigue?"

"I suppose I could help. I haven't had much chance to experiment."

"Did your mother have abilities, too?"

"Once. Before she saved me. She found me bleeding out by a river, and said she sensed something great in me that was worth saving."

So far, Cassia hadn't had much opportunity to prove that "greatness," besides healing a few minor ailments and getting herself wrapped up in this plot with no promise of success. "By transferring her powers to me, my mother sacrificed having them for herself."

"Where did the powers come from?"

"My mother used to attribute them to the Maker. I suppose it's like any ability. Some people have more strength, or skill, than others."

"It's not like any ability I've seen."

"It's true, I've heard of no others like us living. My mother was given her power by a healer before her who has long since passed. Her theory was that one healer exists at a time, and, when they find one they count worthy, they transfer their gift to a new generation."

"So you were worthy."

"Apparently." Cassia looked down and shrugged. "I hoped we'd have more time together to talk about all of this."

"It's tragic, how we only realize what we've had when it's gone. Then we look around, and we have nothing."

Their shared pain oozed into the blackness of the night, the conversation dying into reflection against the popping of the fire.

4

After an unsatisfying breakfast of berries at dawn, Guy and Mack fell into their daily sparring practice. They had so little time to attempt to catch up with the king's knights, so, though it exhausted him, Guy arced his blade upward toward Mack's sizable girth, only to be blocked by his elliptical shield.

Immediately, Guy swung his sword in the opposite direction, but Mack halted the blow with the staff of his axe. Mack plunged his wooden buckler into Guy's middle, knocking the wind out of him.

There was a soft gasp, and the men turned in the direction of Guy's tent. Cassia was there, in the same mud-colored, loose-fitting gown she wore yesterday, her hair newly braided and tied with a leather cord.

"Don't worry," Guy said, wanting to soothe the alarm off her face. "It's better we pick up bruises now than make mistakes in a fortified castle."

"You'll both have to get close to the king to do the job. I don't think you'd stand a chance in a one-to-one fight with his soldiers."

Guy swiped his sweaty curls off his brow. "Thanks for the vote of confidence."

Cassia stepped forward. "May I learn?"

"To fight? Why?" He tried to picture her slender arms wielding the weapon it had taken him years to master.

"If I'm going to be plotting against the king, I want to be able to defend myself. Whether I'm close to the action or not."

Mack plunked his axe to rest in the weeds at his feet. "She has a fair point. Perhaps she can spar with Roland."

"No." Guy protested against that vision. He didn't like the idea of Cassia fighting, but as eager as Roland was, Guy would rather train her himself than leave her with someone who might not be as careful. "All right. Take my sword." He extended the hilt to Cassia. "You'd be more likely to come across one of these than that brutish axe Mack loves throwing around."

Mack just smiled and put his staff in Guy's outstretched fingers. Guy flipped the curved side of the blade towards himself, though he doubted Cassia's strength during the match would be great enough to put her in any real danger.

Cassia took Guy's sword, weighing the metal in her two graceful hands. Then, she backed up into a defensive stance.

"First, you must always be prepared to—" She knocked the axe out of his grip with a swift swing before he even eased it in her direction.

"Sorry," she said, eyes wide. "I don't know what came over me."

"No problem, it's natural to feel nervous." Guy cleared his throat and retrieved the weapon. Nevertheless, he held the handle a little tighter. "Anyway, if an enemy approaches, you must be ready to—" She disarmed him again, with the force of a lioness. There was no hesitation in the angle of her blade or the balance in her right arm.

He picked up the axe a second time and tried attacking in the opposite direction. She parried. He went high, he went low. Finally, he stopped. "You tricked me. You've been trained in swordplay."

"I haven't. At least, not that I remember." Her eyes glazed over for a moment before she dug the tip of the sword into the soil, frustrated. "I experienced memory loss after my accident. But my mother wouldn't have approved of weapons training. Where would I have acquired a weapon, anyway?"

"Where indeed?" he wondered.

"Who cares where she learned it? This is great!" Mack guffawed. "Two more hands in our defense. Now stop your yapping, and prepare to go to town."

"You're leaving?"

Guy heard the panic in the heightened pitch of Cassia's voice. "Come if you wish. We must move on soon, especially since there have been soldiers in the area. I'm just going to market, to gather more provisions for the journey."

"With what money?" Cassia crossed her arms.

Mack said, "Ya can't be squeamish about this mission you've signed up for. We left scruples behind long ago."

Guy cut in, "We're not stealing from the townspeople." He pulled out a leather purse attached to his belt. "My grandfather had a few family heirlooms he was able to take with him when he fled."

Cassia gasped at the sight of the sparkling jewels inside, but Guy tucked it back into the folds of his tunic.

"I'm committed to making this work. What need have I of these things, anyway? They are only reminders of the difference between us and them."

"Why haven't you put these toward your father's debt?"

Guy's face crumpled. "He forbade it, saying that the crown had taken enough from his family, and begged me to pass them on to my own children. The thought. Children born into today's world have little hope for tomorrow. There is more need for a just king than for fancy baubles and bobs."

"Can I come?" Roland strode up, his hair dripping wet from splashing it in the stream.

"You can help us pack up camp," Mack said, his tone boding no argument. "They'll draw enough attention with those fine jewels. We don't need our whole rabble descending on the fair." He regarded Cassia and Guy. "You'd best pluck one of those rings out and pretend to be a married couple who have fallen on hard times."

Cassia opened her mouth to protest, but Mack reminded her, "Leave your scruples behind."

Guy dug into the pouch and produced a golden band. Its gems were a trio of rubies, with the center ruby protruding above the two smaller ones. Vines encircled the stones, making them look like a glistening bed of roses.

He handed the ring to Cassia, not wanting to cross the bounds of propriety with the intimate feel of sliding it on her finger. He was uncomfortable enough with the charade as it was.

Maybe one day he could open himself up to dreams, that he could find a woman to settle down with, in a land where he could support her. Until then, he had to be single-minded.

"So," Cassia started, in an attempt to break the ice that had settled on her and Guy's travel. Her boots kicked up brown clouds on the dirt road. "What is your name, good husband?"

She wished they had opted to take two of the band's four horses to arrive at market more quickly, but the weather was fair, and the walk wasn't terribly far from their camp. At least, that's why she hoped they traversed on foot. Not because the rebels had stolen their mounts and did not want the horses to be recognized.

Guy looked heavenward, at the sun now planted firmly in the top of the skies. "Duke of Sumerson, a reclusive Northerner who desired to try a more temperate climate. And you, m'lady?"

She stared down at her scuffed shoes. "Well, I know at least one villager, so it's best if I keep my own name and pretend you came down to sweep me off my feet."

"Or my money did." Guy laughed.

"What's left of it," she corrected. "You don't look like a pampered palace prince."

He clutched at his chest. "We were attacked by bandits on the way back home, leaving me with naught but these filthy rags."

Guy certainly could bring a smile to Cassia's face. "You're too skilled at making falsehoods."

"A skill quite useful for conspiracy." Guy sighed. "I didn't used to be this way."

"We all make choices based on what misfortunes have met us." How Cassia hoped she was making the right choice now. "I jest, I don't judge."

"How much do you remember from your childhood, if you don't mind me asking?"

"Nothing." She picked at the gaps in the weaving of her basket's handle. "Shadows and glimmers and dreams I don't know are real or imagined."

"Your mother didn't know anything about your past?"

Cassia sighed. "She claimed not to, but sometimes I wondered. I suppose now I'll never find out the truth."

"That must be frustrating. I always try to focus on the task at hand, rather than things I cannot change. But the thoughts rise again, unbidden."

Not only was Guy handsome, kind, and humorous, he was wise and open. For her first long-term contact with the outside world, Cassia had found a treasure among men to share her thoughts with. "At least we have a small quest to focus on now. I always did love going to market. I would go alone to gather supplies. I drew less attention there than my mother, with her strange coloring." Cassia was pale-complected, but Aline seemed completely ashen after the power transfer. There was no blending in for her.

The hush of remembrance for the dead fell over them, but soon forest shifted to field, and then to civilization. Permanent shops crammed together came into view, as well as temporary booths, where merchants hawked their wares, calling out discount prices and expert craftmanship.

Horse manure and an increased number of townspeople added an unpleasant undertone to the sweeter scents of baked pies and roasted pheasants.

They walked in between a humorous juxtaposition of a woman selling fine silks and a man selling a rough-looking goat, thrusting themselves fully into the market square.

A platform for public assemblies was the centerpiece of the market, but Guy took her arm and headed to the baker's stand.

"Cassia, it's good to see you!" Ben wrapped up a fresh loaf in a piece of cloth and placed it in her basket. "On me. For my ear. I've been hearing much better now."

"I'm sure you have," Guy muttered, before Cassia elbowed him.

The baker's eyebrows raised in recognition. "Why..."

"I'm sure you're wondering who has the arm of this beautiful young lady," Guy cut him off in a voice loud enough for the candlemaker in the next booth to hear. "I am the Duke of Sumerson, come to spirit away the most vibrant lass in Lynebrook."

The baker's eyes turned to Cassia in concern, but she simply nodded. "I've found the one I can be happy with. Mother is thrilled that I'm settled." She lacquered Aline's title with honey which concealed the tightness in her chest. "She's moved on ahead of us to prepare the estate, and my husband is humoring our need for our favorite local goods, while we can get them."

"Of course. I see."

Cassia wondered how much the baker knew of Guy's plot, but at least outwardly, he seemed to accept the story. He said, "Well, I wish you much joy." In a lower tone, Ben whispered, "And be careful. We saw a king's patrol come through our lands but a day ago."

The reminder of the soldiers' betrayal struck through Cassia's chest, but she merely replied, "Thank you kindly." The shrill cry of a horn tore her attention away from the baker, who had been a temporary reminder of her and Aline's old life. It was funny, how Cassia had always longed for change, and it now had been thrust upon her in the most jarring way.

Guy's muscles tensed under her arm. Cassia had never seen Lord John of Westcombe before, but based on Guy's reaction, and the fine velvet of his cloak, it could be no other.

He was a short, fat man, surely fed by the sweat of the peasants. The despicable turkey. Had he known of Cassia's mother's assassination?

A much taller bailiff followed behind.

Lord John spread his arms. "Greetings, my people."

Instinctually, Cassia wrapped her fingers around Guy's wrist, communicating caution. Guy had always been perfectly attentive to her, but now his eyes screamed murder. The pulse of hot blood from the vein in his temple distracted her, and she sent a little relaxation his way. She had to be careful, though. She didn't want to be swooning in the middle of the market. That wouldn't exactly be keeping a low profile.

"I wanted to share the good tidings with my subjects that I have been invited personally by Chancellor Radomir himself to the king's annual masque. He has invited all the preeminent lords in the realm, and even beyond, as a sign of good faith in the face of a looming threat in the form of Lancily." Titters echoed among the crowd.

"But fear not. Your benevolent leaders have things well in hand." He looked around, as if expecting a round of applause or flowers thrown at his feet, instead of the grim faces of labor-worn peasants.

"Hmm," he said, drumming his sausage fingers across his midsection. "Carry on!" He threw his arms up once again, as if he were the cause of this joyous gathering of tradesmen. Buyers and sellers gladly returned to their stations.

"Thank you again," Cassia said to the baker as she pulled Guy into an alleyway. He still seemed frozen with rage. She prodded his shoulder. "What happened to leaving the past behind and focusing on the mission?"

Guy flexed his fingers a few times. Without meaning to scan his physiology again, her gift sensed the tingling of adrenaline within them. "Sorry," he said.

"I have an idea."

"You've been having a lot of those lately."

"All good ones. You're lucky I joined the team. Now, you need to get in the palace. What time would be better than when strangers will be descending? When knights will be sodden with drink and too jolly for chase?"

"The Duke of Sumerson attending the feast," Guy said slowly, catching the vision. "From a remote Northern castle, hearing about the need for troops and wanting to band together for our lands' common welfare."

"Not that you'll want to volunteer this story if not asked. The holes will abound. But it's a far better plan than you and Mountain Mack scaling the battlements."

"There's no way Lord John will recognize us. He's too busy blustering to pay attention to faces in a crowd. Plus," he took a step back, studying Cassia. She folded her arms self-consciously.

"What?"

"We'll be transformed, of course. An unrecognizable new couple. My grandfather talked about palace life enough that we can blend in."

"For a moment, perhaps."

"One moment is all we need. One moment to get close to the king."

5

On a leap of faith, hoping that the others would approve of their plan, Cassia and Guy had returned to the seamstress they'd seen while they were walking into the fair and purchased clothing befitting the nobility with the lion's share of Guy's family jewels.

Surprisingly, the merchant had also produced a selection of half-face masks to match, explaining that, though few of her customers had the privilege of attending the king's annual masque, the adornments became wildly stylish at this time each year. Guy left Cassia a single strand of family pearls to wear to the celebration, so she didn't stand out as homely.

Once Cassia tried on her new gown back at camp, she couldn't imagine how anyone could think the wearer of such a gown could be homely, even without a single ornamentation.

It was a bright blue, form-fitting in the bodice with a satin sash which emphasized her waist. Slashes of purple shone through the slits in her tight sleeves. The dress was hardly scandalous by noble standards, but knowing she would be drawing the attention of her companions made Cassia want to remain in Guy's tent forever. Nevertheless, she pinned her thick hair into the matching purple lattice, secured the ribbon of her silver mask behind her head, and stepped into the fading daylight.

Her eyes met Guy's across the camp, and he looked as if he'd never seen another woman before. He wore his newly-purchased green doublet and matching mask, which made his eyes gleam forth like shards of jade, and a golden circlet. Then, he started to laugh.

"What's so funny?" she spat, deeply uncomfortable.

"At least if I die, I will have seen a maiden as fair as you."

"Oh please, be serious," she said, though she wanted to believe he thought her beautiful.

"You two sure are pretty enough to be a part of the royal court," Gisella remarked. "I'm glad you came along, Cassia. They wouldn't let my big brute of a husband in a royal banqueting hall."

"I could pass for a lord," Roland crossed his arms.

"You'd be too busy drooling at the savory meats," his father shot back. "Now. What do you know of dancing?"

"My mother never allowed me to mingle with the public, unless absolutely necessary." It felt like a betrayal, to feel the familiar twinges of resentment toward the woman who she missed so much. But now, having seen the world's cruelty, Cassia understood more than ever why Aline had kept her close.

"There may be dancing at the feast, so it's time we practiced." Mack retrieved a tambourine from his and Gisella's tent and eased himself down on a tree stump. "Everyone, circle round."

Roland, Gisella, and Guy fell into line around him.

"You too, Stephen, this circle's too tight. Come, Cassia."

Guy gave Cassia a hesitant smile and extended a hand so that she could join in between him and Gisella. She took it, finding his grip pleasantly comforting, and was glad he couldn't sense the jumps in her pulse as she could his.

Mack started shaking and pounding the tambourine in a lively beat, and Cassia laughed as the others started to skip in time. It felt so light-hearted and free, like she was the child who had all her memories intact. In fact, the song Mack was warbling sounded familiar.

Then the verse turned to the chorus, and the dancers swiftly changed directions, shocking Cassia. She stumbled into Guy, who hoisted her up so she could regain her balance. She caught on the next time the direction changed and followed along as the dancers weaved in and out of one another, exchanging hands.

Finally, the music stopped, and Cassia had a moment to catch her breath. She hated the mystifying precipice she returned to so often, where it felt like she was returning to something she should know, but she couldn't put her finger on it. Couldn't summon the sounds or skills or people or places that had been her beginning.

She shook her head before it could begin to ache and smiled. "Sorry. I got it there, at the end!"

"Just try not to start out like an aimless wraith," Mack said, and Gisella tsked. "You finished well," he acknowledged.

It was hard not to feel odd, as the girl who healed people miraculously, yet didn't even know how to dance.

"What else do I have to know to enter the court?" she asked Guy.

He was all energy and assurance. "First, we'll be checked for weapons. We'll kneel upon entry to the main hall. You must wait for the chamberlain to direct us to our seats. Keep your eye contact subservient when approaching your betters, and do not approach them without permission. Your equals, you may bow to, but we must keep all conversations short."

"How will I know if someone is my equal?"

"Anyone who looks as if they may topple over from the weight of their jewels, you need to stay away from. It's better to assume a person is your better than to potentially insult a reputable lord or lady." He stuck a finger out. "But don't acknowledge the servants."

Cassia pressed her fingers to her temples. "I think I'll retire now."

Her head was spinning with all the new information. And as beautiful as her dress was, she was unused to such restrictive attire. She surely was not getting enough air.

"Fear not. I'll be beside you every step of the way," Guy said. "Sleep well."

Cassia nodded clumsily and walked away as quickly as possible.

Maybe she was unused to conversing with those outside her family as well. She'd have to learn not to feel so self-conscious. Particularly under the watch of a pair of emerald eyes.

After they sat around the fire, Mack stoked the smoldering embers with a stout stick. Then he brandished the stick at Guy. "You're not going to have trouble playing the role of the doting lover. Just make sure you keep one lovesick eye on the objective."

"I don't know what you're talking about," Guy protested. "Of course I'm focused on the objective."

"Pay him no heed." Gisella wound her arm around her husband's. "Guy deserves to be happy and be thinking beyond an assassination."

Guy took off his mask, relishing the cool night air on his face. It was a blessing that his identity would be better concealed due to the theming of the king's feast, but he did not look forward to wearing it again. "I'm not thinking about anything beyond freeing my father."

"It's not wrong to want other things. A lady can be a great benefit to your life, to soften your heart and strengthen you during your weak times." She poked Mack's side and he nodded his agreement.

"I know that." Guy said. "Just...not now."

"Love hardly waits for the convenient time."

Roland paused from pacing around the fire, in his typical pursuit of constant motion. "You've been away from civilization for too long, Mum. Sitting here making matches on the eve of battle."

"I'm just using the sense the good Maker gave me."

Mack leaned forward on his seat atop a tree stump. "I wonder, though, how far Cassia's power goes. Did she say anything to you on your trip to town?"

Guy didn't know why he felt disloyal to divulge Cassia's confidence. She was a part of the group now, but he still felt the strange urge to protect, and to keep a part of knowing her to himself. "It sounds as if she's capable of nearly anything. She passed out when we first came upon her after healing my wound, however. The power exhausts her."

"I wonder if it's like our sparring, if it may improve with practice. It sounds as if her mother hid her away for good reason."

Guy didn't like where this conversation was going. "Cassia has role enough in our plot. We're putting her in danger with the charade. She will help us if we're injured."

Mack leapt to his feet. "But what if she could maim just as easily as she could stitch together? Think of the possibilities. They would never see that coming. They wouldn't even be able to attribute it to us."

Guy rose too, to flatten Mack's enthusiasm. "Until she falls to the floor in a heap!"

Gisella shushed him. She whispered, "We don't want to disturb the poor girl's rest with plans of doing the unthinkable, without her consent, no less."

"It only makes sense," Mack continued in a lower tone. "Our plans were shoddy at best. Then I wouldn't have to sneak in at all to support you. I'd just have to be nearby. It's beginning to feel like we have a chance."

"We'll talk to her in the morning. And respect her decision," Guy warned.

Mack sat back down and said, "Of course." But he smiled like he'd already won the fight.

"You're insane." Cassia gripped the rough sides of her skirt.

Guy shrugged. "Possibly. What's the problem? You liked the idea a minute ago."

"I liked the idea of taking down Peter. Not you."

"Just give me a scratch. Or a sting. Whatever you feel inspired to do."

Cassia raised her eyebrows, not sharing his apparent sense of humor about this situation.

"I'm not afraid of you," Guy said. "You have to practice, or we'll never know what you can do."

"Maybe you should be afraid."

Guy's expression grew serious. "I promise, you cannot hurt me in a way that can't be fixed. I'm strong. But if it will be too hard on you —"

"I'm not worried about myself. I guess I can't be a part of the plan if I don't practice, but I don't like this."

"Think of it like our weapons training. We have to know that you can target someone in combat. You should have a successful experience to draw from, even if you can't go full force yet."

"What if I can't control it?"

"I believe that you can." The left side of his smile twitched in amusement. "Unless you hate me that much that you won't be able to resist."

She scowled. "Keep teasing me and I might."

The truth was that Aline had said as little to Cassia about her abilities as was practical, and now Cassia was expected to have perfect command in a life-or-death situation.

Cassia closed her eyes and took a deep breath. If she kept doomsaying, she'd never have the courage to begin.

It wasn't hard to sense Guy. She'd been trying too hard not to these days. She imagined a small abrasion, burning across Guy's forearm.

She felt it work, as well as his sharp intake of breath. She opened her eyes. "I'm sorry." It felt so wrong to hurt rather than to heal. She started to reverse the damage she'd done right away.

"I'm okay." Guy ran his fingers over his skin a few times until the red retreated. "Wow, that's amazing."

She yawned and his attention turned to her face. "How are you?" he asked.

"Okay. A little drained," she admitted.

"Understandable." He gestured to the grass. "Let's sit. Do you think you'll ever be able to do this on a larger scale?"

"It doesn't feel natural now. But believe me when I say that what's pulsing under the surface for the king is anything but health."

"My arm," Guy hollered. Where the abrasion had dissipated only moments before, a deep and angry red welt now festered.

She had inadvertently recreated his wound, and larger this time. "I'm so sorry. I didn't mean to hurt you. I was thinking of *him*." She healed Guy as she spoke, and sank against a tree, her breath measured.

"That's a good sign." He gulped. "Maybe I'm not as tough as I thought. I should get Mack to volunteer—this was his idea."

Cassia bristled. "I don't know. I don't want to put everyone at risk."

"We signed up for risk. Now it seems you're the key to our plan."

She frowned. "I've never been a part of anything. I'm not sure I'm the best one to rely on."

"I have faith. The Maker has granted you power, and we are using it for a righteous cause. I'm sure He will smile upon us."

Cassia crossed her arms. "You are?"

"What, do you not believe? After experiencing such power as you have?"

"Such power? I'm not certain it will be enough."

"We've only just begun. Just picture a smug king at the end of the road."

Cassia dug her fingers into the grass. "I'll picture my mother, who never deserved such a brutal fate as this."

"On second thought, maybe don't picture it now. Wait until you have more control. I'm not eager to have my arm split open more than once per day. I'm only human."

"But am I?" Cassia turned to his generous eyes, hoping for affirmation. What she found shocked her. Admiration.

"It's true that I've never met another person as gifted as you are. I am, however, certain that you are good. You are talented. You are unlike anyone I've ever encountered."

He leaned closer, and Cassia was aware of Guy in a wholly unmedicinal way now. Then, Roland strolled into the clearing with a bucket of water.

"Do you all want me to leave?" he asked.

"No, no, we're done for the day. With training." Guy pounced to his feet and helped Cassia up, but he did not meet Cassia's eyes again. Why not? For modesty's sake? Or did he realize he shouldn't be attracted to such a strange, sheltered girl?

She shook her head. The mission. Truly, she was addlebrained. She didn't share Guy's faith in the Maker, or in herself. But her rage, she had absolute confidence in.

6

"Alessandra wouldn't have wanted this," Cristian said.

Peter threw his silver goblet at his younger brother's face. The projectile fell short, but the liquid painted a wine stain like blood down the front of Cristian's doublet. The cup clattered off the edge of the raised dias and rolled to a halt on the straw-covered floor below. "Don't use her name around me."

"We're all still feeling the loss," his brother amended, hands out in contrition. Good.

"You don't feel it as I feel it."

"Of course not," Cristian said. "Though her family, no doubt, suffers greatly."

Typical. Cristian was always trying to undermine Peter's pain. Peter tossed the remains of his bread roll down, having lost his appetite.

He leaned forward, meeting Cristian's eyes across the table. "If you knew the depth of my sorrow, you would not be throwing it in my face now. You would be supporting me, instead of accusing me of being manipulated."

Cristian pulled at the ends of his sandy hair. "I am trying to support you. I simply think you are not in the state of mind to fend off attacks against yourself."

Peter stood. "You would accuse your king of being weak, Brother? Paving your way to the throne, are you?"

Hurt flashed across Cristian's face at the implication. But Cristian had one thing right. Attacks had come, from every direction. From those Peter had thought he could trust. And no one, not even his own flesh and blood, was above suspicion when it came to ensuring the success of the nation.

"Do you have interests in Lancily?" Peter continued. "Is that why you cry against war so boldly?"

Cristian stood as well, stretching to his full height, though it was two inches shorter than his older brother's. "I have interests here, in Lynebrook. And I would not see her so easily weakened for a war of no profit."

A servant from the hallway eased the door open with a creak. "Your Majesty. Radomir is here to see you."

"Good, bring him in. Maybe he can get Cristian to see sense."

"I'm sure he can, with that gilded tongue of his," Cristian muttered.

"Watch yourself. I am not pleased with your attitude."

Cristian dipped his head, but the tense lines remained on his face.

The servant held the door open for Radomir, who strode forward, his dark cloak fluttering majestically behind him. Peter had to admit a smidgen of envy at that special, unteachable talent Radomir seemed to possess of commanding whatever room he entered. Maybe the advisor's confidence would one day rub off on Peter. Until then, he craved his shrewd counsel.

Peter invited them all to sit back down at the head table. "There's been some doubt as to the necessity of the coming war." Peter left Cristian's name out of it. Despite his bluster, he was not yet eager to see his brother thrown out of the kingdom.

"I see," Radomir said, assessing Cristian anyway. "As I've told you, Majesty, Lancily is a clear threat to our posterity. They grow in numbers and in reputation with our neighbors. They've had the chance to make allies of us, yet they stubbornly remain independent, caring nothing for our laws and traditions."

"Quite right."

"Let not detractors cast shadows over our glorious plan. There will be many who will whisper in your ear, trying to curry your influence to their own interests. But I have never yet led you astray."

He smiled and his graying hair and many rings glimmered in the candlelight, bringing to mind Cristian's nickname for Radomir: "the silver man."

Peter folded his arms against the shiver that came over him. Perhaps he should also get himself a cloak, to sweep around behind him in the more drafty parts of the castle.

"Guard," he called toward the hallway with authority, though he was a little embarrassed he could not recall the man's name posted outside the door. "This fire needs bolstering."

"I'll send someone to you right away, sir," the knight's muffled voice promised.

"You were there for me, Radomir, when no one else was." Peter shuddered at the memory of how weak he'd been. Hardly the picture of a determined king, but Radomir had helped shield his grief and frailty from the public eye until Peter had pulled himself together.

He was mostly sure he was whole now, though sometimes when he breathed, he swore he could feel the air seeping through the seams of his hastily-soldered pieces. "We must keep the state strong, at any cost."

Cristian opened his mouth to protest but closed it at Peter's sharp glance. He would suffer no more opposition. Not from his baby brother, or anyone else.

Sunlight streamed over the bluff where Cassia stood feeling the soothing breeze. The wind whipped her fine skirts about her legs. She couldn't remember a time she'd felt so comfortable and free.

Two muscled arms wrapped around her stomach, and she turned in glee to find the golden-haired boy. She threw her own arms around his shoulders, and they kissed and kissed. She felt so close and secure, and wanted to stay there forever, but then she remembered why he'd come.

"Enough of this."

His hands slid down her arms to clasp her hands. "I could never have enough of this."

"Yes, but then what would we get done all day?"

He put on a mock-serious face. "You are most important to me."

"You promised to help me with my shooting."

He sighed and looked down at a small boulder beside his feet, behind which he'd safely planted a bow and arrow before surprising her with them.

"I didn't know how hard it would be to keep such a promise when you look like an enchanted woodland fairy, recharging her powers in the light."

"You believe in enchantments now? I do doubt your judgement."

"It's all your fault. There is magic in the world that had never been there before we fell in love."

His endearments were hopelessly over-the-top, but still, Cassia relished them. She shoved him playfully and rolled her eyes. "There was plenty of magic in the world, you were just too dense to see it."

He dropped to his knees. "Promise never to leave me so blind again?"

The sight of him on his knees pledging the world to her was an intoxicating prospect, but she pulled him up with a groan. "Yes, yes. Now help me with my shooting."

She plucked up the smooth bow, and adrenaline pulsed through her veins at the thought of improving her craft. "I'll surpass you, one of these days."

"I have no doubt," he smirked.

Cassia's eyes opened, not to a pair of hazel ones, but to the white canvas wall of a tent. A cloak was balled up underneath her head, protecting her from the stabbing straw which prodded the rest of her body on the uncomfortable tick.

She knew she shouldn't complain. When had she ever had the luxury of a finer mattress, especially in a temporary camp where her protector slept on the ground outside?

It was simply this horrible feeling of loss. The loss of her own mattress. The loss of her precious mother, which she kept shoving down, knowing if she would face it, Cassia would stop functioning. Her inability to remember what were dreams and what were true memories.

If what she'd dreamed was a memory, then where was the golden-haired boy now? Was it witless of her to miss a young man she'd never truly met?

Cassia peered out of the tent and realized that Guy was no longer resting beside the fire. It was midmorning—she'd slept in again—and Guy and Mack were diligently conducting their practice rounds.

She really had to become a useful part of the camp, to gather supplies and prepare meals like Gisella or train with the men. Gisella was nowhere in sight, so she headed for the sparring pair, although she was still a little shaken from her inexplicable display the last time she joined them.

Remembering her dream, she asked Roland, "Do we have a bow and arrow?"

He eagerly left his post observing the older men and headed into his tent.

When Cassia saw the weapon, even as used up as it was, the same rush of adrenaline filled her veins. Of course, the adrenaline sparked colder and clearer now that she could sense every chemical in her post-healing body.

"What do you usually shoot at?" she asked.

"Tree trunks. Sparrows, if I'm lucky enough to spot one." He brushed the back of his hair with his hand. "I'm not the best shot, though."

"I think..." Cassia paused, frustrated at the lock in her brain. "I think I might be able to help you."

Roland looked skeptical, but, to his credit, he didn't argue with her.

She notched the arrow and pulled the string tight. It felt natural in her hands, like a part of her.

Just then, a quail soared through the sky. She pierced its heart within seconds. She knew she had without looking, having an awareness of the bird.

"I'm sorry, friend," she whispered. She was a practical woman, having survived off the forest's gifts to save precious coin, but she had no joy in killing the beautiful creature.

Roland whistled. "That will crisp up nicely in the fire tonight." He looked over her shoulder, and Cassia turned to see why.

Mack and Guy had ceased fighting and were silent. They had come to terms with her strange healing powers, but this new revelation seemed to shake them.

Guy formed all his questions into a single word: "How?"

Cassia dropped the longbow. "I promise I'm telling you the truth. It's just like the other day. I don't know how I can do this. I don't remember."

Mack blurted out, "It seems as if in your past life you were trained as part of the royal guard! I've never seen a woman with such skill."

"Maybe she should take Peter down with an arrow, rather than with a look," Stephen suggested.

"No. Too dangerous. Her other skill is more stealthy," Guy said.

"At least a bow and arrow is something I can understand," Stephen grumbled.

"I'm happy to help, however I can." Cassia wished they'd stop talking about her, though she understood why she would be a topic of fascination, as odd as she was.

She'd always longed to distinguish herself, to become a valued part of society, but not like this. Half of the party looked more inclined to lock her away than to celebrate her. Perhaps the sheltered life she'd lived thus far had its benefits.

Gisella burst into their company, a pile of dripping laundry in her arms. "We need to be moving on. I just saw a bailiff's patrol by the wider part of the creek."

Stephen hurried to deconstruct his tent, and Guy and Roland followed suit while Mack took the bundle from Gisella. "Did they see ya?"

"No," she sniffed, and he thumbed a tear off her cheek. "I climbed a tree and put the clothes around my shoulders. They never did see the water droplets running down the trunk."

"That's my clever woman. Now let's gather what we can and get going. These are no king's soldiers, but it could be that the bailiff's got wind that we looted a battlefield."

"Or are no longer paying taxes," Guy added.

"Or are planning to masquerade as the nobility," Roland threw in.

The crew packed up what they could quickly strap to the horses while Cassia scattered the remains of their fire. Soldiers were chasing them.

Part of Cassia wanted to turn around and face anyone sworn to be loyal to the king, but she had a job to do. One that could slip through her fingers if the bailiff's men caught up with them.

Guy mounted and patted his horse's chestnut coat. "Cassia can ride behind me, on Aurora."

Cassia froze in protest, but Mack called out, "Our course is set. There's no use delaying any longer. Let's be on our way."

Cassia grabbed Guy's outstretched hand and mounted behind him, scooting as far back on the saddle as possible.

"When is the king's feast scheduled?" Roland asked, now astride his own horse beside Stephen's dappled steed.

"Three days from now," his father answered. "That should give us plenty of time to loosely follow the main road."

"Let us pray that nothing else happens on the way." Gisella wrapped a scarf around her damp shoulders, though it was midday, and shivered.

She swung up behind Mack on his bay, who was snorting with excitement after many days of confinement. Then, they rushed off to start their long journey.

After a day and a half with no sign of danger, they slackened their pace. "Cassia," Guy said. "Do you think you could practice healing while we ride, or would it be too risky? I know we were going to start working on your endurance before the feast."

"It depends on what I need to heal. If it's something small, I think I can sit on a horse." Cassia didn't want to continue to harm them so she could practice. It felt barbaric, and she didn't want to weaken them by causing further injuries. But she could reach out to each of them. Maybe they had some existing ailment she could fix.

Sure enough, she sensed a curving in Mack's spine. That wasn't small, but she could try. Reluctantly, she ceased gripping the sides of Aurora's saddle and locked her arms around Guy's midsection to gain a more secure posture.

At her silence, Mack looked over. "Cassia, what are you doing? Cassia?"

"Keep your seat."

"What—"

Cassia rolled his vertebrae into alignment one by one, like strands of flax around a distaff. He cried out and sweat ran down his neck, but then, he straightened. Moved his torso from side to side. Healing was always gratifying, but it was especially so now that Cassia could take credit for it.

"Does it feel better?" she asked.

"Yes. Thank you." The higher pitch of Mack's normally gruff voice betrayed his astonishment.

She nodded, but then her chin dipped down to rest in the hollow between her collarbones.

Guy shook her awake. "Cassia?"

"Hmm?" she said, slipping back into unconsciousness.

She woke to warm, strong arms pinning hers down. She furrowed her eyebrows before realizing that Guy had wrapped her arms around his waist again to keep her from sliding off Aurora.

"It's not safe to stop and rest yet. Can you remain where you are?"

"Yes, don't worry," she protested, even as her head jerked forward, this time plunking between Guy's powerful shoulder blades. That woke her up a bit.

Cassia was glad Guy couldn't see her face flush with a rush of red-hot blood. He was so handsome, and so concerned about her. An image flashed before Cassia's eyes of the golden-haired boy before she shook it free. The present situation was confusing enough.

They both tried to maintain a proper distance, but she tired quickly of keeping her spine so rigid. The steady canter of the horse caused her alertness to slip again, until her head fell pleasantly into the crook of Guy's neck, and sleep claimed her.

Guy was glad that Mack was in the lead. It was hard to concentrate on navigating spare branches, let alone navigating a safe course to the royal palace.

What was all too easy was enjoying the tickle of Cassia's silky hair against his neck. It still smelled of campfire smoke. In sleep, she seemed completely trusting and relaxed with him.

There was understandably always an edge to Cassia. She had lost her family, her memories, and was at the mercy of strangers, some of whom had regarded her with suspicion at first. She seemed to doubt herself deeply, even though she was supremely gifted.

Now, reclining on his shoulder, he could imagine she needed him. She was counting on him to look out for her.

He laughed at the thought. The woman could heal ailments with a thought. She didn't need anyone, let alone a peasant like him.

Of course, she was a peasant, too. But her simple tunic couldn't hide the majesty that she exuded from within. She would catch any man's eye.

The tale they'd spun about Cassia being swept away by a rich nobleman was all too probable. It would be easy enough to act his part. Then, it would be time to stop pretending.

For the first time, the thought of life after the plot seemed a little glum.

Guy blew out a breath, controlled, so as not to wake Cassia. Though the woman could sleep like the dead.

He had bigger things to worry about than his growing attraction. He wasn't certain about having Cassia deliver the killing strike. She'd only just joined, at a time of deep personal anguish. Her gift was untraceable, but she still could get caught up in an investigation.

As much as the thought of dealing the fatal blow himself sent a dagger of nerves plunging through his heart, he would rather do so than expose Cassia to so much danger. He would rather leave her outside altogether, but it didn't sound like that was an option anymore. Mack was thrilled, Cassia was willing to risk it all. As they all had decided to be.

He supposed, should she faint in the act, it would be easy enough to blame her anxiety upon seeing the king. However, rumors could fly when disaster was afoot.

Cassia stirred against him, stoking fires of tenderness in his heart. Then she sat up, and the cool air that blew through his tunic in her absence was like reality whirring his mind back to sense. Stay alert.

"Have you been to the palace?" Cassia asked.

"Mack has. There's a portcullis, which will be wide open to admit guests to the feast. It may not stay that way once the king is slain."

"We'll have to move quickly, to avoid being captured and questioned, then." She sounded as methodical and level-headed as always.

"It is only logical to think that the guests will want to flee at the sight of bloodshed, contention, and confusion. We'll make our escape the moment the deed is done."

"So much is left up to chance."

Gisella entered their conversation. "It's the last prayer of the desperate." Her voice was tired.

She was rarely pessimistic, but she hadn't failed to make clear her feelings of her husband and son risking their lives for the chance of a better one. Grief made some let go of all inhibitions, and others hold on all the tighter to the people they still had. "Do you think we've gained enough distance to make camp?"

The sky was ablaze, and the sun had nearly set. Mack answered, "This is a good place. Plenty of cover. I'd judge we're a day away from the royal city."

They reigned in their sweaty mounts to give them a well-deserved rest, deciding to only construct a simple fire and sleep under the stars, rather than unbinding all their poles and tents.

Gisella passed out strips of dried beef, and the crew sipped from their waterskins. They divided the second-to-last loaf of bread. Even after the provisions, Guy's stomach rumbled, but they would need to save what they'd been able to salvage.

It was risky to interact with people when they were traveling like vagabonds, but the danger only increased the closer they got to the castle. Guy and Cassia could not be seen as dirty, haggard peasants, but as traveling nobility.

In fact, it was good they were on course to arrive near the palace grounds late on the morrow, as it would likely take all of the morning after to scrub away the filth of outdoor living.

Guy offered Cassia his blanket to bunch underneath her. "I'm sorry about the accommodations."

"Nothing I'm unused to. Are you sure you don't need this?"

"I'm fine." Feeling a heady sense of satisfaction as she snuggled into the wad of fabric, he laid down and tucked his arms under his head.

Despite the descending chill of night and the fact that she'd slept so much on the journey already, Cassia's eyes soon fluttered closed.

Guy had slept outside her tent, mere feet away, before, but it was different, being able to see each wisp of hair tumbling out of her braid. To witness the deep rise and fall of her chest. Then a tear rolled out of the corner of her eye. She was crying in her sleep.

Gently, Guy smoothed his thumb over her cheek and wiped the

drop away. He brushed her creasing forehead with the back of his fingers until it relaxed.

She certainly had enough to process, losing her mother and home so recently. Plotting regicide. He wondered if, in her dream, she was recalling one of those hazy memories she once told him about.

Guy turned away. He would never sleep if he stayed staring at Cassia, trying to understand all her secrets. But turning away didn't feel right, either. He flipped back over, wanting to have a direct eyeline if anyone were to approach her from behind. Guy hoped that Mack wasn't watching, waiting to rebuke or tease his wool-headedness again.

Mack had been correct on one point—Guy wouldn't have to try hard to act the part of the doting lover.

7

After another day and night of frantic travel, the time had come for Guy and Cassia to dress for their charade. Cassia's hair felt so soft and light down her back after a good scrubbing in the river. They were about a league from the castle.

When darkness fell this evening, they would join the main road, hold their heads high and convince everyone they belonged there. Suddenly, hiding in the muck of the woods didn't seem so bad.

She cried out as Gisella fashioned her locks into a tight chignon.

"Sorry, love. Just think of me as your lady in waiting." She laughed. As if either of them could obtain such an exalted position. "We can't have your hair falling over your shoulders in the middle of a dance." Gisella pinned the net into place and dropped her reassuring hands to Cassia's shoulders. "My. You are a pretty sight."

She flipped Cassia around for a hug, and the feeling of being cared for brought tears to Cassia's eyes. How she missed her mother.

Gisella rubbed her back. "There, there. Are you feeling all right with all of this?"

"Yes. I want to end the king's oppression like he ended my mother." The harsh words felt shocking coming out of Cassia's mouth, but they felt like absolute truth. "If this is the time, then I'll have to adjust, whether or not I feel ready."

Gisella nodded. "I admire your determination. I simply worry that you're acting out of emotion, not out of conviction. You just lost your mother. No one would blame you if you needed to wait. Regroup. Think."

Cassia shook her head against Gisella's shoulder. "No. If I think too much, I'll fall apart." She straightened. "I'm not as brave as I seem. I have to push through this act of the selfless vigilante, as well as the invited noble now, if I will ever have justice for her death."

"Okay. You know your own mind, I'm sure." The creases beside Gisella's eyes showed her reluctance to let go.

"Ready?" Guy's voice boomed, and Cassia turned to face him. His dark brown curls shone and bounced beside his verdant eyes, and his doublet emphasized his broad shoulders and impressive arms. He was breathtaking.

Even more intoxicating was how his eyes held hers, as if she were nothing less than captivating. Then, he cleared his throat and looked at his worn boots. New shoes were an expense they had not been able to incur. No matter. No one would be staring at Guy's feet. At least if they were female.

"I'm as ready as I'll ever be." Cassia took his arm, and Gisella's eyes twinkled at the sight.

"You've secured your weapon?" Guy asked.

"I have." Cassia patted the dagger concealed under her skirts.

Cassia knew from their plan that Guy also had a dagger strapped to his arm under his sleeve. He would check in his grandfather's sword at the door, as was the custom for feast days, and hopefully come back out with it.

Mack, Stephen, Roland, and Gisella would only have the bow and the ax for protection, should danger arise. Roland was a better shot than Stephen, so he was the designated archer, with Stephen left with naught to battle with but his hands. So much was left up to fate.

Cassia pushed down the dread in her stomach and stood straighter. She was no whimpering peasant tonight. She was the Duchess of Sumerson. And she would have her revenge.

As she and Guy approached the castle, arm atop arm, Cassia was glad the other nobles seemed determined to dismount their horses in as grand a state as possible and have their masks, clothing, and jewels in every color of the rainbow be admired. No one noticed one more couple walking up with little ceremony of their own.

Torches glowed on the pathway leading to the open portcullis. A shiver of foreboding ran down Cassia's spine as she entered the gaping mouth, looking up at the iron grate that would be sure to close them in if they made a mistake. Guy flipped his downturned palm upward to grip her fingers for a moment of reassurance.

In the castle courtyard, Cassia's eyes flicked to the first set of chambers to the right. Guy had mapped out what would likely be a rough layout of the fortress yesterday. Sure enough, the opening was to a gatehouse, with guards pouring in and out of it like blue and orange clad locusts. Cassia looked away. A duchess wouldn't pay attention to such things. They instead followed the crowd to an arched doorway straight ahead, with guards stationed on either side.

She gave the men a nervous smile, then stole a glance at Guy's stoic expression. Right. She oughtn't acknowledge them either.

The great hall was lit by a series of chandeliers. It was so difficult not to stare up and admire every detail. There appeared to be engraved patterns of phoenixes in the metal, gleaming a glorious gold in the candlelight.

The radiant illumination made the walls, painted in a clean white, shine. Now and then the wash was interrupted by an exquisite tapestry.

"Perhaps these were woven by the king's mother," Cassia whispered.

King Peter's parents had been killed on the road many years before by vagrant commoners, though this in no way excused the king's reign of terror.

"Whoever wove them, the royal family paid for these fine materials with our toil and tears." Guy's voice, though low, was dangerous, and it was Cassia's turn to squeeze him back into their performance.

When the line of nobles finally inched forward enough to allow them to stand beside the grand marshal, Guy called out the fake titles they'd invented.

"The Duke and Duchess of Sumerson," the grand marshal said with a flourish. "You are very welcome. Please, have a seat next to the dais." The next set of peacock partiers descended. "His majesty will be honored with your presence."

Cassia nodded and moved toward the tables and benches near the king's throne, pretending to be thrilled that their titles had earned them a seat so close to where the crime would be committed. She and Guy should have aimed for a less conspicuous, lower social status.

The middle of the hall was cleared for dancing. Atop the tables were navy runners, candles, and berry garlands. It was a wonder the servants had had room to decorate the centers, what with the hundreds of silver cups, trenchers, and the food.

Roasted chicken, fresh fruit, sweet confections—many dishes she had never laid eyes on before, that were undoubtedly many days' worth of wages, sat for their consumption on the table.

"Imagine, needing a cushion to rest your rear end on. Think of all the pheasant juice and ale they will soak it with before the night's end," Guy whispered. They sat down and dipped their fingers in the washing bowl.

"It is strange," Cassia replied, though the vitality and beauty of it all captured her more than she cared to admit.

The plump noble across from her had already tucked in, though he managed to sneak appreciative glances at her in between mouthfuls. Guy must have noticed the same thing, for he scooted closer to her.

Cassia took hold of a glistening haunch of meat and ripped some of the juicy skin off to put on her trencher. The taste was divine. The cooks had crusted it in dried parsley and sage and cooked it to be perfectly tender. For her next portion, she dug in a little less daintily.

Guy was surely hungrier than she was after living off of traveling provisions, yet his restraint reminded her to act the part of a well-fed lady, unamazed at any delicacy she encountered.

By the time their trenchers were emptied, the hall had filled completely. Cassia followed the leadership of her tablemates and wiped her greasy hands on the linen tablecloth. How would the palace laundresses ever return it to its fine white condition now? A few staccato blasts from a horn, and the room stood at attention.

Heads bowed and knees curtsied as the marshal announced the entrance of their king. Cassia's stomach clenched as she clutched her skirts and showed reverence to the man whose troops had murdered her mother. She'd never felt such depths of anger. Surely she could sprint across the room in a moment and choke the life out of the pompous royal ruler.

"Steady," Guy breathed. "Collect yourself."

Cassia slowly drew in air through her nose, the aromas of the food now nausea-inducing rather than tantalizing. She swallowed, hoping that if anyone looked her way, they would assume she was overwhelmed with awe for their sovereign instead of hatred. She had to be in control. There would be no second chance.

A pair of opulently-dressed lords trailed the king and stepped onto the raised dais. Then, two ladies joined them, their raven hair contrasting against the platform's rich blue canopy. Cassia's gaze snapped to the younger woman. "Laurel," she whispered.

"What?" The spell was broken for a moment by Guy's hushed exclamation. He was regarding her with thinly-veiled panic from the corner of his eyes.

Cassia looked back to the dais, where the favored nobles were taking their places behind the high table. She ripped off her mask to regard the king more closely. His hair had grown, his skin had freckled with sunspots and worry lines, and his jaw had filled out. But she still saw the boy of her dreams. Of her memories.

"Peter." She said his name like a prayer. "Peter!" she called, stumbling her way to the dais.

Guards closed in on Cassia from both sides. A scuffle behind her caused her to turn and see two of them detaining Guy, who had raced to her rescue. Oh. She wasn't supposed to approach or even address the king. And certainly not by his given name.

"Alessandra?" The elegant woman Cassia now recognized as the mother who'd cared for her for the first sixteen years of her life. Elaine was squinting at her, no doubt recognizing Cassia's features but not the silvery sheen to her hair.

And yes, that was Cassia's father beside her, and her sister, who must be the age now that Cassia had been when she disappeared. Over the past six years, Laurel had transformed into a striking young woman.

The mighty, severe king's countenance had blanched. "This cannot be."

Cassia could hardly feel the pull of the guards on her arms, as delighted as she was to see Peter and her family again. "It is I. I have only just remembered."

"Cassia?" Guy asked, his voice strangled.

Her new name, like the warm, strong spice that grew from the earth, felt sweet and real. Her former name, Alessandra, had too many loops and flourishes. It sounded like a court dance, an exquisite painting. Not a girl masquerading as a duchess in a pretty dress.

Cassia turned to face Guy, wincing at how the shock had seemed to transform to disgust as she did not deny a connection to the royal court.

Peter stepped forward. "Who is this man?"

The threat to Guy reminded Cassia that she spoke, not with her childhood love, but with a king who had proven himself to be both commanding and cruel. "He's my friend. He's been looking out for me as I made my way to the castle."

The grand marshal cleared his throat.

"Speak," Peter said. His voice had become deep and resonant in the years which had passed.

"When these two entered the hall, they claimed they were the Duke and Duchess of Sumerson."

"I didn't know if you would agree to see a woman who claimed to be back from the dead," Cassia lied quickly.

"And how did this resurrection happen?" Peter's shoulders were firmly set, but a hesitant hope flickered behind his eyes.

"The healer," she whispered, sobered by the memory of the life drained from her mother's eyes. Or should she say, from Aline's eyes? "You had her killed?"

Peter clenched his hand into a fist. "I didn't know what she'd done with you! Only that she had failed to revive you and disappeared, without even a body to leave me to mourn and honor."

"She wanted to keep me away from you. She had a sense about people." Cassia swayed on her feet, the memories of how deeply she had loved Peter slamming into how she had resented his neglect, persecution, and heinous acts.

"Alessandra." Peter tested the name out softly before clearing his throat. His next words were more firm. "Clearly you need rest. Your mother will escort you to a guest room until your quarters can be...refreshed." He turned to Guy. "Thank you for your assistance. We'll take care of Alessandra now."

Guy was breathing heavily, trying to maintain an even

expression. No doubt concealing feelings of utter betrayal.

Cassia wanted to explain, if only she could. Peter was right about one thing. She needed to close her eyes, be still, and process all that had happened. Would she be permitted to send Guy a message once she recovered?

Her mother—yes, she knew the Lady Elaine, though thinking of her as "mother" felt strangely discordant after so many years of living with Aline—approached and gently guided her out the stone doorway the royal court had entered through. Her fingers trembled. "Alessandra. We are just as shocked as you. If we'd only known, we'd never have ceased searching. We've missed you so." Their footsteps echoed through a corridor that seemed like it should be foreign, yet, was strangely familiar. Just like her dreams.

Cassia remembered running down these halls, one time knocking a painted hanging from its peg on the wall. Always teasing Peter, even when they were older, and their games shifted from hide-and-seek to stolen kisses.

Her cheeks flamed at the memory, and she shook her head vigorously. That could never happen again. Not unless the boy she thought she'd known could be unearthed once more.

"My room," Cassia said with surprise as her mother slowed after turning to the left.

"His Majesty hasn't allowed us to touch it since you've been gone. I'm sure it's in a terrible state now."

"His Majesty?" Was Peter insistent on her parents using formal titles, though they'd known him since his infancy?

"We'll put you in a room further down. Still close to your father and I."

Cassia knew that thought should bring her more comfort, but she was still struggling to recall all the feelings of familiarity. She longed for the open air and rough tree roots where she could breathe and clear her head.

The suffocating sensation intensified once her mother opened the door. A mattress, so plush it was doubtless stuffed with feathers instead of straw, sat upon a four-poster bed. A luxurious rust-colored bedspread covered the mattress, and the same material was also draped like a canopy around the headboard.

"This is a guest room?" Cassia asked. She approached the window and brushed her fingers against smooth glass. It, too, had a fabric curtain. Beside the window was a roaring fireplace. She would never be cold again. Her head pulsed. She would never be cold again if she stayed.

The window overlooked a square courtyard with a fountain within. Just beyond that lay the woods where her band of dissenters had lately gathered. Surely they were on their way back home now. To regroup? Or had she dashed all their hope forever?

"I'll send a maid with a change of clothes." The sound of Elaine's voice jarred Cassia back to the present.

"No! I mean, thank you, but, could she please come in the morning? When I've had some time to rest?" If Cassia had to maintain her statuesque composure a moment longer, she felt sure she would crack right down the middle of her rigid smile.

"Of course. The washroom is just in there, if you'd like to clean up a little before retiring." Elaine gave a nervous nod and fled the room.

Cassia collapsed atop the made bed, not wanting to sully good sheets with her nervous sweat, and was asleep within moments, flashes of memories before and after her healing warring in her mind.

8

"I insist on being present." In Peter's study, Radomir stroked his silver rings with long fingers.

"You can hardly be present when I have dinner with my long-lost love for the first time in six years."

"Forgive me if I am thinking less about romance and more about the safety of the kingdom," the chancellor deadpanned.

"Alessandra is not a threat to the kingdom." Though Peter had his suspicions at first, he refused to let Radomir tread this far. She looked strange and bewildered, to be sure, and something could be done about the frightful color of her hair. But no enchantment could have concocted the familiar lines of her face. It was as if, all this time, he had known she was alive.

He had poured his passion for finding the healer into the wrong purpose. If he hadn't been so easily convinced by Aline's lies, he and Alessandra could have saved so much wasted time. What had it been like, to be trapped with a witch all those years?

No one would rush them this evening, and he intended to find out. He'd seen a flicker of love in Alessandra's eyes, though marred by confusion. He would gain back her admiration, and it would be as if nothing had changed.

"Your Majesty," Radomir said with infinite patience. "You're not thinking clearly. You've had quite the upset. You need someone rational, a friend, to find out what she's doing here. What her true feelings are."

"Her feelings are unaltered."

"Perhaps." Radomir didn't outright correct Peter, but pursed his lips nonetheless. "What if I were to be concealed, within hearing? That way I can counsel you, add my opinion to what you hear. We can't afford to show any weakness whatsoever on the cusp of our great victory."

"True. You make much sense Radomir, as usual."

The one false tooth in his smile glinted as he smiled. "That's why I'm here."

Cassia's young maidservant, Gionna, had scrubbed her with lemon-scented soap and dressed her in an amethyst gown with thick, rich fabric which rustled when she walked. Her hair had been plaited with ribbons and wound underneath a finer net than the one she'd come in.

Cassia had outright refused the heavy set of jewels that came as part of the ensemble. The rainbow of magnificently stitched gowns that had been expediently delivered to her wardrobe over the course of one day was already enough of an adjustment. Guy's pearls and ring felt like a shield against the unfamiliar.

The more Cassia saw of the castle, the more she felt she was simultaneously coming out of her fog and retreating back into it with the shock of her former life. Gionna had informed her that the castle had two dozen chambers within its walls, where notable and celebrated guests of the king were welcome to reside.

Cassia hardly needed an escort to make the brief trek back to the great hall, but didn't raise a complaint. Even conversing with a deferential and unfamiliar escort was preferable to the uncomfortable reunion which awaited her. Cassia knew her anticipation of speaking with Peter should be all positive, but it wasn't.

The creak as Gionna swung open the door to the dining hall seemed eternally long. Then she heard "Alessandra." Peter leapt up from his chair to greet her, an honor Cassia was sure wasn't extended to all of his guests. She nodded to her new (old?) name a half second too late.

"Peter...it's good to see you." She hoped it wasn't disrespectful now to call him by his given name.

He seemed only reassured by the informality. "Please, sit. I've arranged for us to have a private meal to catch up." He looked to the attendants standing at attention, their backs to the walls. "You'll be served mead, wine, anything you'd like."

"Cider would be fine if you have some, thank you."

They sat as they were served, and the silence hummed. It felt odd to be in a place of honor beside him when they'd lived apart for so long.

"Do you still enjoy hunting?" Cassia asked, desperate to break the awkwardness.

"I do. Just the other day, I struck down a boar as big as a pony."

She dipped her head in admiration, unsure if that was an accomplishment she used to admire. She'd shot countless animals, but in the quest for survival.

"How are you feeling?" he asked. "Are your chambers sufficient? Would you like to be moved into your own room?"

"I am perfectly comfortable. Maybe I can visit my old room tomorrow to help me gain my bearings."

"So, you do remember your life here?" He scooted to the edge of his brazen throne.

"I don't think I ever truly forgot. But the past seems blurry. Obscured."

"I'll answer as many questions as you need." He glanced almost nervously at the floor-length curtain behind him. Odd.

"There is something I'd like to have clear. You see, I've heard that your people are overtaxed. On the brink of starvation." Of course, she'd not only heard about but seen the devastation firsthand. The question was, how much did Peter know about it?

Cassia declined her chin and leaned her face closer to better study his. "Is that true? Isn't there any way we can help them?"

Peter's eager expression grew as cold as stone. "Who told you that? That man who brought you to the castle?"

"No," she said, a little too adamantly.

"You always did like to give me a hard time, but surely you trust my leadership more than this, Alessandra."

"I didn't think it could be true, so that's why I wanted to know how people could get such ideas." She worded her response carefully.

Guy would be proud of her restraint and subtilty.

"What was that man's name again?"

So Peter couldn't be diverted from his jealousy. He was either more intuitive or more suspicious than when last they met. Cassia forced her face into a neutral expression. "Guy."

"No title? And where did you come across this Guy?"

She answered, "In my village," since a sickly feeling in her gut told her that if she lied, he'd only find her out and question her more. She had to get notice to Guy, to protect him if he was foolish enough to return home.

What was she thinking? Of course he was home. He would never abandon his father, though she had abandoned their plans. And her interest in him had the power to end him for good.

On the subject of petty retaliations, Cassia wanted to ask about Aline, but Peter's change in countenance cautioned her against it.

They feasted on steaming meat pies, eggs peppered with chopped dittany and fennel, syrupy pears, and thick, crusty bread. She wondered at how soft the inside was and how it came served with sharp slices of cheese.

Peter watched her fascination curiously. "Alessandra" simply hadn't known how blessed she was to have such luxurious foods, and in such a great quantity.

He expelled a heavy breath. "What a hard time it seems you have had."

"It wasn't so difficult. I didn't know where I came from, so I was mostly content with where I was. I read often. Spent time outdoors."

"That reminds me, I've arranged a picnic so that you may reconnect with your family."

"Oh. Thank you." It was thoughtful, but Cassia's nerves grated at the fact that Peter kept planning things without asking her input. It was true, she was all mixed up inside, but having every detail of her days planned out for her wasn't helping her adjust.

Peter seemed to struggle with his words for a moment, before saying, "You remember we always intended to marry?"

Cassia stiffened. "I remember, but I certainly don't feel ready for that right now."

"I understand. But we are not as young as we once were. I hope to see you as much as my schedule allows, so that you can remember your love for me and restore our routine."

Cassia smiled wanly and dipped her head, then took a long drink of cider. She stayed as long as was polite, pretending to be engaged in his talk of rowdy peasants and dull administrative responsibilities, when she was actually panicking on the inside. She excused herself, claiming the fatigue that she was still truthfully feeling.

Which action would be correct? Who was safe and who was lying? Aline? Guy?

Her newer friends felt more trustworthy, but how could she base her decisions on an identity that had been crafted for her without her knowledge?

Or was Peter, her doting former love and the tyrant king, a better protector of her interests? Was he capable of change? And would Cassia ever come around to a vision of her future that she no longer desired?

Instead of retiring to her chambers as she'd said she would, Cassia knocked on the door Elaine had pointed out as her own. Her mother looked surprised, though pleased, that Cassia had sought her out.

Cassia stepped inside and closed the door behind her. She didn't remember everything about Elaine, but she had the feeling her mother was a discreet woman. "I need to write a letter, to the friends who took care of me when I was lost. I want to let them know I'm all right."

"Of course," Elaine said, retrieving a quill, inkwell, and paper from a writing desk. She was giving, too. More images flashed. She had always been there when Cassia scraped a knee after playing too roughly with Peter and Cristian, or to comb Cassia's hair back and turn her warrior child into a proper little lady of the court.

Cassia smiled at Elaine, and joy broke forth on her mother's face as she took a seat on her bed. Cassia moved to Elaine's writing desk and composed a letter to Ben the baker, explaining as best she could the events of the last few days without outright expressing her fears that the king was a danger to them, in case the note was intercepted. She hoped her wishes for their friends' safety and prosperity came through the hastily scribbled words.

Her pulse jumped at the thought of Guy reading them. Of his disapproval and distrust.

No matter. She had to try and warn them, and hope they reached back out. Her mother assured her she would send a messenger with the note on the morrow.

The next day at their family picnic, Elaine, Laurel, and Jadon were warm and kind, but definitely on-edge. It almost put Cassia more at ease, to know that she was not the only one who wanted to make a good impression as they got reacquainted.

Elaine's dark hair was streaked with white, and her face was starting to crease, but her burnished bronze eyes still shone with kindness and beauty. Cassia tried to recall if, before her healing, she'd also had brown eyes.

Two servants had unrolled a soft blanket for them to rest on, and Cassia leaned back on her elbows, relishing the refreshing breeze.

"How has the adjustment been thus far, moving back into the castle?" Elaine asked.

The simple question lowered the floodgates and released the burden weighing down Cassia's heart. "I don't know how to fit in here, or if I ever will again. I'm sorry."

She looked at how her family would respond to her outburst, but Jadon's—her father's—smile was warm and contagious. "You are still our courageous, outspoken daughter, that much is clear."

Elaine replied, "In time, you will find your way again."

If Cassia only knew which way was hers. "In truth, the castle makes me uncomfortable." It seemed a stone fortress, and the man holding the key was the man Aline had warned her about for the past six years.

"You've lost your love for the king?" Elaine whispered, her eyes full of worry.

Their attendants were standing a respectful distance away, but Elaine's hesitance to speak freely only strengthened Cassia's own fear. She lowered her tone to match Elaine's, and her sister and father leaned in closer. "I can remember that I loved him, but now he seems like someone else."

Jadon's face was tight. "People change much in the span of six years."

Cassia frowned. "And what I'm getting to know, I do not like."

"Perhaps you could be a gentling influence on him?" Laurel

suggested. Sweet, innocent Laurel.

"No," Jadon said firmly. Now that Cassia was spending time with her family, memories of his determined care for her were coming back. No one interfered with Jadon's two girls. "On the path Peter has chosen, it is more likely that his ways will overwhelm Alessandra, and not the other way around. He has closed himself off to all sane advice."

"So how can I make my own path?" Cassia sat up straight, desperate for the answer.

"We always have a choice. We just have to decide if we can reconcile ourselves to the consequences which follow," Jadon said gravely.

What would Peter do if Cassia never came around to loving him? He had appeared patient so far, but how long would it take until his patience ran out?

Elaine pulled up on the silver chain of her necklace, and the pendant's charm appeared above her bodice. The metal was crafted to look like the curving branches of a great tree. "We must trust in the Maker to watch out for us and guide our steps."

Cassia's anger flamed. The way Cassia saw it, this Maker had a strange sense of humor to determine that her whole life should be stolen away. She was glad to have known Aline and a less privileged way of living, but where was He when Aline was murdered?

"Please, put that away," Jadon hissed.

"You don't believe?" Cassia asked him.

"Of course he does, but we aren't allowed to openly, because of Aline," Elaine answered, tucking the tree back into her dress. "She was such a devout follower while she lived in the castle, and when you disappeared, Peter was so angry that he disavowed anything having to do with her."

"In the villages, some still believe in a Maker. I suppose villagers are further from Peter's hand."

Elaine sipped from her goblet. "That is good to hear."

"So, you knew my—" Cassia stopped short of saying mother, not wanting to hurt Elaine's feelings. "You knew Aline well?"

"I did. She helped me birth the two of you," she nodded to Cassia and Laurel, "and cured me of many ailments. We talked much about the Maker's tree, the tree beside the crystal rivers of water. She had a theory that the tree was an actual place, the source of her advanced ability to heal." Elaine picked at a bunch of grapes. "We had planned to make a trip there together one day."

She met Cassia's eyes. "I never believed that she'd intentionally done you harm or stolen you away for a heinous reason. Perhaps she was scared of Peter's pull on you and had her reasons to be."

Elaine appeared to shake off the heaviness of her recollections. Aline's decision had had severe repercussions for not only Cassia, but for her entire family. "Now that's in the past. How is Aline doing now?"

"She's dead," Cassia answered shortly.

Elaine gasped, but Cassia didn't want to dwell on the topic. She was learning too much about her late mother's secrets to quit probing now. "You attribute Aline's strong aptitude for healing to the Maker's tree?"

"I do. Or the waters that run beside it."

Cassia had intentionally said "strong aptitude," mimicking Elaine's description of Aline's abilities.

Aline must have concealed the extent of her powers to the royal court before her escape, likely for Elaine's safety as well as her own. Elaine did not appear to know that Cassia could heal broken bones with a glance, and Cassia was glad for it. It was a secret which could hurt many if the wrong people got wind of it.

But could the older courtiers start to suspect, based on Cassia and Aline's similar coloring? Or would they merely assume her changed appearance was the cost of a near-death healing, instead of the mark of a new life?

"At any rate, I'm thankful you had someone to take care of you. Even if it couldn't be me. And I am thankful you are here with us now." Elaine clasped Cassia's fingers, and Jadon and Laurel's smiles promised that they felt the same. At least Cassia had a few friends in this intimidating castle.

9

Guy must have had a death wish. Why was he riding back toward King Cutthroat when his shoddy plan had dissolved into shambles? Only to talk to Peter's lying bride-to-be. Guy had delivered her right back to his door. For all Guy knew, she had written to him on the king's command, as a trap.

If only he could get her off his mind, and accustom himself to a life of laborious, unjust poverty. It was infuriating, the hopelessness of another assassination attempt now that he'd made his face known. Yet, he worried for the girl with the gossamer tresses, who looked as stricken and helpless as a peasant child when her noble heritage was announced.

If Peter had hunted Cassia's mother, did he know about Cassia's own abilities? Had he been kind to her? Maybe Cassia could advocate on behalf of the farmers, though Peter had hardly proved willing to listen in the past.

The truth was that Guy's goal had shifted from only caring about a change in leadership to making sure that Cassia was all right. So here he was with another half-baked plan, settling back on the outskirts of the royal grounds and waiting for a servant to exit who hopefully would bring his message to the king's betrothed, rather than their sovereign himself.

He caught a young boy on his way to town to deliver a missive, clutched in his small hand. The boy looked devoted enough in his task for Guy to hope he had no proclivity for telling him lies or blackmailing him for a reward.

Guy stepped forward onto the cobblestones which paved the way to the palace, hands extended in a placating gesture. "Excuse me, young squire. Can I trouble you to deliver a message to the castle when you return?"

"Squire? I'm just an errand boy." But he looked pleased with the increase in title, and the glint of coins in Guy's outstretched right palm.

"Do you know the Lady Alessandra? I'm an old friend from her childhood home."

The boy's face lit up. "I know her. Everyone's been talking about how she's returned. She's not like other grownups. She likes to talk to children."

Guy produced an envelope from Aurora's saddlebag. "I would be much obliged if you'd bring this letter to her."

"Why don't you give it to her yourself?" He shifted his feet.

Guy decided partial honesty might be best than subterfuge. The lad wouldn't want to risk a threat to his employers. "I don't want His Majesty to get the wrong idea, like I've come to court the lady. I just want to let her know I'm in town, if she wishes to come and visit." He popped open the wax seal for the lad to read for himself, before figuring that the young one likely couldn't read a word.

Regardless, the boy studied the lines as if he could understand, and then seemed satisfied Guy wouldn't show him if the message was one to do harm. "I'll bring it to her."

Guy waited for hours in the shadows of the trees until darkness fell, jumping at every sound of an approaching person. But the servant boy must have fulfilled his promise, because under cover of dusk, Cassia emerged in the flickers of palace lantern light.

He was cowed at her fine styling and dress for a moment, before looking into the face that had been the subject of many an unwanted meditation over the past few days. He felt her healing presence with her gaze, though he hadn't realized he was unwell until now.

"Wouldn't it have been better to come during the day?" Guy asked. "Won't the guards suspect?"

"I've taken to walking around the castle each night," she

answered. "It helps me go to sleep. Makes me feel less caged." She wrung her fingers together, and Guy remembered her fitful nightmare the night her mother died. "But we'd best not linger too long, lest someone comes to investigate. Peter is...quite curious about any of my activities since we've been separated."

A pang of jealousy and bitterness stabbed Guy. "So that's that, then. You'll return, because nothing he's done matters to you anymore." Guy was so used to feeling alone in the heat of his determination, his sense of injustice towards Peter. Now he'd found someone to care about, and she'd fallen prey to the same cruel master.

"Of course it matters." Her intertwined fingers balled into tight fists. "I just have to tread carefully."

He crossed his arms. "Now that you have a lot of fine things to lose."

Cassia's soft tone morphed into an indignant cry. "Like my life and family."

"Yes, I wouldn't know what it means to still have that." Guy could logically see her points, but emotionally, he'd felt the urge to lash out and hurt as he'd been hurt. But the wounded expression on Cassia's face splashed cold water on his anger. He took a fortifying breath. "Forgive me. I wouldn't want to put you at risk."

She shook her head. "You're right, I seem like a hypocrite. But, hurting Peter doesn't feel right anymore, even after all he's done. I loved him once."

"And you don't anymore?" Guy asked hopefully.

She took a peek at him through downcast eyes. "I can't say that I love him when people are suffering, and he's so concerned with his own image that he won't hear protests to the contrary. However, I don't believe he was always this way."

"Perhaps. Or perhaps you were blinded long ago by young love and privilege."

Cassia gripped Guy's forearm. "I believe there is still good in him. He is kind to me."

"He has much to gain by being kind to you." Why couldn't she see through Peter's manipulations?

"True. And yet, I can't leave all this behind without learning more about my family. About myself."

"And he'll let you go, then? If you decide you no longer want to remain in the castle and marry him?"

A lightning rod of fear flashed across her eyes before she clenched her jaw. "He'll have to."

"He'll have the means to stop you, if he wants." Guy swallowed hard. "Why don't you come with me, now?"

"Part of me longs to, but I'm just not ready. I need more time."

"I'm afraid your time is up." The arrogant drawl Guy'd first heard at the feast issued from the road beyond the tree line.

"Peter—" Cassia started.

"Don't." The king, in full battle regalia, came into view and Guy charged forward, infuriated at how Peter disregarded Cassia.

Peter simply turned to the line of guards behind him. "Slap him in irons."

They rushed in and he was bound, hopelessly outnumbered.

Cassia pleaded, "No, he's my friend."

Peter pulled at his gauntlet, unmoved. "No friend of yours should be inspiring you to leave me and commit treason and insurrection."

"You're acting like a tyrant," she spat.

Peter straightened. "Put the lady in a cell as well." He turned to Cassia. "I have been too soft with you. Some time in the dungeon will teach you your place."

"You're mad." Guy struggled against the hold of two knights, but they forced him to his knees. How had he and Cassia become so engaged in conversation that they'd allowed themselves to be ambushed in such a way?

"Stop, Guy," Cassia said. Her guards had not cuffed her wrists, but they held each of her arms, and she looked impossibly small between them. "You'll only make things worse for yourself. Peter will let me go eventually or risk the wrath of the court."

Peter was studying the stars, as if he was not the one giving the order for his loved one to be locked away. "Dealing in threats, are we? Something you must have picked up from this slum runner."

Though Cassia was surrounded, she threw her shoulders back and looked every inch of a warrior queen. "You used to like when I'd stand up for myself. What happened to you?"

She finally hit a nerve. The king spun to face what he was doing. "I lost you before. And I'm still not sure who I've found."

Her face was stone. "Whoever's speaking poison in your ear isn't you. And since you used to value my advice, I'd recommend you stop listening to them."

Peter turned his back once more. "Take them away."

10

"You shouldn't have come." Cassia's cell was adjacent to Guy's, so they could hear each other but not see each other. They each sat near the bars to more easily converse.

"You'd still be a prisoner if I hadn't. The difference is, now you know you are one."

"I could've used my fireplace, though." Cassia's tone was teasing, not accusatory.

Guy rattled his bars. "I'll get you out of here."

"How? We haven't any tools to break the door down, or to fight off a dozen guards."

"Haven't we?"

Cassia considered the question Guy had posed to her in the forest. She hadn't told Peter about her new abilities. How could she, after he'd reacted so poorly to a change as minor as her developing a conscience toward the peasantry? How much more outraged would he be to know Cassia had powers far greater than his control, powers that she'd received from Aline?

"I don't know, Guy. If I'm not strong enough to manipulate even one person we encounter, we'll be caught, and I'll really be on the executioner's block." Peter was trying to bully Cassia into submission, but so far, he was treating her hints at rebellion as a childish lark. Something told her taking down his royal knights wouldn't be perceived so gently.

Still, she had the opportunity to free Guy. There was no doubt in her mind that Peter would be rid of him as soon as possible, without a second thought.

"I think you can do this if you're willing to try. If not, I understand. I was wrong to accuse you before. You need to look after yourself." The intensity of Guy's statement injected Cassia with comfort and warmth.

Once again going on the offensive went against everything Aline had taught her: to reach out and help others with what she'd been given. But as foolish as it seemed, Guy made her want to be fearless.

Cassia sighed. "Healing a cut is one thing. I've never attempted to subdue the mind. The control center of the whole person."

"Maybe it will be easier than repairing a number of tissues, to only take hold of the most powerful region of the body. Try on me first."

"Don't you tire of being experimented on?"

"I hardly have anything to lose. Stop worrying, Cassia."

He was the one risking his life, but she was the one who had to deal with the guilt if she failed. Yet, he'd given her consent. Even more so, urged her to continue.

"All right." From the sound of his voice, Cassia pictured Guy sitting behind the left half of his cell bars. Then, she was looking out upon the dingy dungeon wall from his eyes. She snapped full awareness back to herself and shuddered. She'd never lost control of her own body but could sense both her own and Guy's perceptions simultaneously.

"I couldn't move for a second." Guy sounded horrified. And a little awed. "How are you feeling?"

"Not as tired as I normally am after using my power." Cassia admitted. "But I'll have to try again."

"Of course. I'm ready."

The second time Cassia reached out for Guy, it was easier. Somehow, she was able to stay seated on her own grimy cell floor while bringing Guy to his feet. She walked him in a circle and sat him back down, testing her command of his fine motor skills by interlocking his fingers. Then, she came back to herself. It was wearing, but doable.

What was more unsettling than physical exhaustion was the sense that she could violate someone's autonomy so completely. Guy trusted her, but it was still sobering to have that level of control over someone.

Cassia's eyes fluttered closed to give relief to her racing mind. "Let me rest for a moment. Then, we'll escape. Don't let me sleep past a few minutes."

Slumber came easily. She would regain as much energy as possible, but they would have to leave this night. They were out of time.

"Cassia." She awoke to Guy's whisper. "The guard changed." Cassia reached out to sense the new young man. It was unsettling, how easy taking over a person's senses had become. She didn't stay there long enough to be detected.

"Okay," she breathed. "I'm going to have to bring him closer to get the keys."

She reached out again, forcing him to walk down ten stairs and toward their cell. She had to take care, as he had locked his muscles in panic, trying to figure out what was going on. She compelled him to use a hand on one wall to steady himself, then marched him right in front of her. Cassia could see her own determined expression through his eyes before she dropped his heart rate, slowed his breathing, and put him to sleep.

She reached her arms through the gaps in the bars to support the fallen guard as his knees began to buckle, taking the brunt of his weight on her own rear, as she hadn't anticipated how heavy the man would be. She checked in with him again. Still breathing, still sleeping.

"I'm sorry," she whispered, though of course, he couldn't hear her.

Sweat poured down her brow, but she had no time to rest. She eased the keys from the loop on the guard's belt, clicked the lock open, and swung the door out so she could unlock Guy's.

"I'm going to scout out where everyone is so I can control as few people as possible." She flipped perspectives from bystander to bystander, not remaining long enough to be detected, in order to commit the less populated pathways back to the nobles' quarters to memory. Running past her family's rooms would not be ideal, but that was the only part of the castle Cassia felt sure she could navigate without becoming lost.

When they ascended the dungeon stairs, however, a vision came of a young Alessandra and her sister, sneaking down the servants' corridor for extra sweets. "Take a left," Cassia stepped past Guy to lead the way. "We can flee out the kitchen."

At the late hour, the pantry was deserted. The grounds, of course, were not.

"There is one guard on patrol, facing away from us. Two on the wall, currently facing outward." She gripped the consciousness of the one on the wall's walkway to the left of the portcullis. "Raise the gate." She whispered the order as they hastened towards the exit.

His companion gave a cry of surprise before she controlled him too. She made him pull the chains with his fellow, but the effort of keeping two scared and strong-willed men in submission made her head pound fiercely. It was double the effort from any healing she'd ever done.

"Don't fall asleep," she commanded herself. Their lives depended on it.

Guy put a reassuring arm around her, even as they hurried faster forward. The gate creaked midway open, and she took over the mind of the knight on the grounds as well, to keep him from overtaking them. Then, all went black.

11

Cassia woke with her face smothered by a heavy blanket and stifled a scream. Had they caught her? She was lying down, jostled alongside waxy wheels of cheese on a rough cart. She slid the blanket down to peek at her surroundings with one eye.

The sun-streaked signs of dawn were above, and Guy, adorned with a rough farmer's cloak, was driving Aurora forward. She breathed a sigh of relief and sat upright. Forest surrounded the dirt road, with no palace in sight.

"You'd best stay under, Love," Guy said. He instantly belied his tender term with a hasty throat-clearing. "The initial set of riders fell for my disguise the first time they laid chase, but they may circle back."

"Shouldn't we abandon the cart and go under cover of the wood?"

"When you're strong enough to keep the pace. They'll have patrols sweeping the trees soon."

Oh. The memory of frantic fleeing from the castle returned to her as swiftly as the leadenness laying her limbs down.

"Plus," Guy continued. "If we abandon the cart mid-road, it will rouse suspicion. Best to drop it on the outskirts of some town."

"Well, if that's all required," Cassia said, her quip slightly muffled under the horrid blanket. She lifted the cover ever so slightly with her fingertip to increase airflow. "Do you want me to see if I can sense anyone down the road?"

"Your energy will be best spent recovering, in case we have to run."

Their casual pace was necessary to blend in but agonizing.

"Did you have all this prepared when you came?" Cassia asked.

"I may have borrowed it from one of His Majesty's sleeping serfs." The levity Cassia had missed so much laced Guy's tone.

Whether the farmer lived off the king's profits or not, Cassia wished they weren't reduced to stealing. However, this was life or death.

The Peter she used to know would never have put her in the dungeon. Had the Peter she used to know truly died with Alessandra?

"I'm sorry you put yourself at risk for my sake. I realize now that I was attempting to belong somewhere that I don't anymore."

"You're always welcome with us."

Cassia was sure the rest of Guy's group was none too pleased with her recent actions, but she prayed they would understand once she explained. "I may just take you up on that offer."

She would miss the chance to reconnect with her newfound family, but she could no longer be lady, daughter, sister, and friend if Peter would forbid her to also be a forager, helper, and healer to those most in need. Would she ever be allowed to reconcile all the parts of herself and make a difference?

The pounding of a dozen sets of hoofbeats sounded down the path, along with the jingling of armor. "Guy," Cassia breathed. She didn't have to reach out to know the soldiers were coming, and it was too late to do a thing about it.

"The king is with them," Guy said, urging Aurora on at a quicker canter.

"Halt!" Peter's cry turned Cassia's blood to ice.

Cassia tried to control the small squadron but felt her consciousness fading away. She was too tired. It was over.

"What am I to do with you?" Peter paced the length of Cassia's bedside.

"Where's Guy?" she croaked, still groggy.

"In the dungeon, with double the guard. He won't witch us again."

So, Peter thought Guy was the enchanter. At least he hadn't killed him the moment he suspected.

Peter met her eyes. "Don't look so smug. He dies tomorrow. I only wanted him to be a public example to those who would defy my divine right to rule and step between us."

In other words, Peter wanted Guy to die slowly, with humiliation.

"I'll never forgive you if you kill him." Her voice shook.

"You love him?" Envy flashed across Peter's face.

"No," Cassia said, though her face heated. "He's a good man. He doesn't deserve this."

Peter huffed. "You are so, so different. So muddled up. I must be forgiving, however. I've waited for you for this long."

Cassia clenched her bedspread with her hands. "I cannot live with a murderer. I will not."

"And if I show mercy, you will?" Peter arched his brow.

Cassia drew in a breath. She had been willing to die to help Guy get his life back. Would she be willing to live with this misguided and cruel man to accomplish the same goal?

The fact was, Peter would hold control over her whether she consented or not. At least this way, she could save Guy. Maybe she could do even more.

"Guy's father is in debtor's prison for overdue taxes. The Lord of Westcombe is stealing from the people. You shall free Guy and the debtors of his region and demand that the ruling lord collect only a fair wage." Cassia lifted her chin, though she trembled inside at the desire to make things better.

He considered her. "Your concern for the poor commends you, though it comes at the cost of loyalty."

"The people would commend you too, if you would lighten their burden."

Peter ran his fingers through his golden hair, still damp from the exertion of the chase. "There are more factors at stake. Once the peasants figure out that they can bargain for what they want, there'll be no end to their demands."

Cassia sat up in the bed, energized with the hope that Peter's defenses might be crumbling. "No one need know of any bargain. Only of a generous king," Cassia swallowed. "And his supportive bride."

She had said the magic words. Peter paused to think only for a moment.

"I will let the cad go free this once, on pledge he will never molest us again. I help his village, and we will marry within the week?"

Cassia nodded firmly, mechanically. "I believe Guy will make such a pledge, if I ask it of him."

"You two will not conspire without an audience," he warned.

Cassia gritted her teeth at the term "conspire." It was true, they had broken Peter's trust, but he had accepted no responsibility thus far in driving his citizens to that point. "Fair enough. I agree to your terms, and thank you, Your Majesty."

A smile lit Peter's drawn face. He stroked her cheek, and she resisted the urge to flinch away. "I knew you would come to your senses. You won't regret this, dearest."

As he swept out of her room to make the arrangements known—swept out of her prison, she corrected the phrase at the sight of a guard on duty outside of her door—Cassia feared that regrets would haunt the rest of her days.

12

Despite their frantic fleeing, Guy still stared out at Cassia from behind bars. She should have known their first escape plan would fail. But now, she had the chance to save him.

"You can't do this. You can't give your life away for me." Tears glistened behind Guy's eyes.

"I can and I must. It's not just you I'll be saving. This is also for your father, and countless others who are imprisoned unjustly. I won't stop advocating for them."

Guy banged his fist against the bars, and it was clear from the way he hung his head that he was seeing reason. "I would take you from here," he muttered softly. "I would that we could—"

"Don't," she interrupted, tears pricking her own eyes. "I must be strong. We cannot think about what might have been. This is what is."

She took a long breath. "For years, I longed to be a part of a community. Now you can go back to your village and look after the friends I've made. Return to them, and know I shall never regret meeting you."

"Selfless to a fault." Guy shook his head. "I'm glad to have met you too. You are truly a special maiden."

Radomir cleared his throat behind Cassia. The snake. She'd forgotten for a moment that Peter had sent him to ensure no other escape plot was hatched.

"You've been granted mercy you don't deserve, you ungrateful peasant. The Lady Alessandra will return to her betrothed now. Do you swear never to return upon pain of death?"

"Please do it," Cassia whispered. "I'll be fine."

Guy looked at her, rather than at Radomir, his passion so intense that it was a relief to turn away once he vowed, "I swear."

Radomir gestured to a guard, who unlocked Guy's cell and led him up the stairs. "And you're not to hurt him," Cassia called as a reminder of Peter's promise.

She took a step to follow before Radomir's bony fingers clamped around her wrist. "Just a moment, my lady."

Cassia snatched her wrist away.

"I'd like to take a moment to make one thing clear. You think you have sway with the king. That doesn't matter, because I am in charge of this castle," he sneered.

"Take care, Chancellor. The king would not like to hear of your disloyal remarks."

Radomir wheezed. "And you are one to talk of disloyalty. The king likes to hear whatever I tell him. So far you are not worth the effort it would take to talk him out of love with you. If you remain compliant."

It was bad enough that Cassia had to tread carefully around her former love. Now another adversary had stepped forth from the shadows. "Compliant how?"

"You will not undermine my authority. You will speak no further on matters of poverty or war that are far beyond your understanding."

Was Radomir the man pulling Peter's strings? This would explain how the king's viewpoints had morphed into something different, something ugly, over the last six years. Cassia planted her hands on her hips. "Or what?"

Radomir leaned close, relishing his threatenings. "Or I will kill your family."

"You would be caught," Cassia bluffed.

"Would I? You stumbled into our midst. Unexpectedly, with an unknown purpose. Oddly changed." He raised an eyebrow. "As blanched as your dead adoptive mother."

Heat spiked beneath Cassia's skin.

"I wonder, if something were to happen to your family, if a

magnificent healing might occur once again?" He grinned. "What would that mean, if the enchanter that was supposed to be far from the castle did not take his enchantment with him? There was only one other by his side during his miraculous escape."

Radomir spun his silver ring in circles around his finger, as if they were merely discussing the weather. "Then who would Peter call disloyal?"

"He will understand, once I explain." Cassia's voice shook with the disbelief of her own words.

"There'll be no need for any explanations. If you behave yourself." He turned on his heel and left her, so secure in his authority that he evidently didn't see a need for further debate.

He had seen Cassia sacrifice her life for Guy. He had gambled on the fact that she would do it again to save the family she used to know, and Cassia had played right into his hand.

Perhaps she should have pretended as if she didn't care what happened to them, but she wasn't willing to take that risk. A man so mad as to threaten the family of the king's bride was a man who was capable of anything. Cassia was even more trapped than she had thought before.

As she slipped on the blue satin dress, Cassia remembered that, from the time she was a young child, she had dreamed of marrying Peter. The gold-embroidered borders shone on her stately, dripping sleeves, and a sapphire glittered like a teardrop between her collarbones, but her girlhood fantasy had turned into a nightmare.

Her mother sat beside her, no more joyful due to Cassia's vacant expression. What mother anticipates her daughter preparing for her union with numbness and resignation?

"Cassia." She rose as the seamstress left the room for more pins. "If the wedding is too soon, why do you not petition the king for a postponement?"

Cassia dropped her arms to her sides, the dress's heavy material reminding her of the manacles Guy had so lately worn. "Peter would never postpone the ceremony. The banns have already been cried, and he would be humiliated."

Elaine clasped Cassia's hands. "A man will go to great lengths for the woman he loves."

Did Peter love Alessandra? Or did he merely seek to recreate the future that once slipped through his fingers?

"This is what is best for everyone." Cassia squeezed her mother's hands, then released her grip to smooth down the pleats of her full skirt.

Though Elaine had become almost a stranger thanks to the gaps in Cassia's memory, she did not want any harm to come to the kind woman who'd cared so well for her. She could show no signs of nervousness around any in Peter's service, should the dressmaker come back in.

"What's best for *you* is what's best for me." Elaine's tone was urgent. "There's no point in forcing yourself to be miserable."

She looked at her mother. Cassia had once sought refuge in Aline's advice. She could tell Elaine was eager for her daughter to trust her in the same capacity. But at what cost to the family's safety?

As if sensing something was wrong, her mother said, "You know you can tell me anything."

Elaine's tender invitation brought back a handful of memories of stroking Cassia's forehead during illness or after nightmares. The desire to be no longer alone caused the truth to burst from her lips. "Radomir said he would harm you and expose me if I refuse to bow to his whims. I feel like I'm promising myself to two unfamiliar, domineering men within a matter of days."

"Alessandra." Cassia's eyes stayed glued to the floor. "Cassia." Cassia raised her head. "You were born a noble. Born to be a queen. But more than that, you've displayed true majesty within your heart with your concern for others, and I couldn't be more proud."

She cupped Cassia's chin in her hand. "But now, it's time to value yourself just as you've valued us. Do as I ask and be liberated from these unrighteous men. The Maker has called you back to your family, and that is a blessing beyond what I could have ever imagined. But I don't think He called you back to subject yourself to slavery. I'm not afraid to die. If it's my time, it's my time."

Cassia's expected path had twisted and turned like a serpent over the past few days. Could it truly be for a purpose, as a benevolent being watched over her from above?

Her mother made it sound so simple. But if Cassia made another mistake, all might be lost. "I will save you if necessary, but be wary.

Send word to me if Radomir tries anything. Don't walk the halls alone."

The seamstress returned then. They'd been speaking quietly, but had she heard Cassia's final words about Radomir? The woman continued with the dress fitting as if nothing had happened, but a weight settled in Cassia's stomach that would not be relieved.

How would she survive the coming days when she didn't feel free to have the briefest of conversations with those on her side?

Surely there were some in Peter's employ who didn't agree with Radomir's tactics, but like her spotty memories, this was simply another obscure piece of information that Cassia could only hope would come to light the longer she lived in the castle.

Showing the boldness of his position with the king, Radomir poisoned Cassia's mother during that evening's meal. Cassia didn't know how he'd accomplished this exactly, but she watched Elaine grab her stomach, then wheeze, and when her mother completely doubled over, Cassia knew she had no choice but to reach out and separate Elaine's blood from the poison now running through it.

Value yourself, Elaine's expression seemed to plead. Cassia no longer remembered every detail of the woman she used to be. But from the beginning of her life to what might be the end, Cassia knew that she upheld integrity and condemned evil. She looked Radomir straight in the eye and healed her mother from the inside out.

After a few seconds of sending the toxins back up Elaine's esophagus, Cassia's mother coughed the deadly liquid back up and spat it into her wine glass. A few breaths later, Elaine looked to Cassia, and so did the rest of their table.

"Why do you gaze at me?" Cassia asked Peter. "Detain this evil man, he's poisoned my mother!" She pointed an accusatory finger at Radomir.

He sputtered. "Your Majesty, she lies. And it's just as I suspected. How did Lady Elaine heal so quickly? Alessandra used her witchcraft on her!"

Peter shifted to face Cassia, and she met his gaze boldly. "It was you?"

She thought about denying the truth and calling them both addlebrained, but who then would Radomir attempt to kill next?

Instead, she gave a slow nod.

"She is dangerous! She must be hanged." Spittle dropped from Radomir's lips and landed on his trencher, his usual composure caving under the fear that Peter would listen to Cassia instead of him.

"Now, Chancellor," Peter put out a conciliatory hand.

Cassia broke in, "I am no danger, and I will not harm anyone anymore. I wish to heal with my power."

"She will not be ruled—she has proven that already. You endanger the kingdom by keeping her around."

"I love the kingdom," Cassia protested. "Isn't that obvious? All I desire is for our people to prosper under just laws, and if that interferes with your agenda to lord over everyone—"

"See? She is questioning your leadership." Radomir's fist rattled the table. "Lynebrook must withstand those who would seek to tear it apart from the inside."

"Yes, Lynebrook must." Peter viewed Radomir as if through new eyes. "It's true, the Lady Alessandra has not been transparent with me. There is much new information to sort through." He raised his fingers to the guards. "Please take her back to her room for the time being."

They hesitated to follow their king's command, no doubt contemplating what Cassia had done to a handful of their fellows the other day.

"Do as I said," Peter yelled.

The men hastened to her side, and she leapt up before they could take hold of her arms. It was frustrating to be treated as a criminal when all Cassia had wanted to do was save Lynebrook. But she had been willing to go too far to do so, and her punishment had caught up with her.

Never again would she justify deceit and vengeful harm as the means to an end. Doing so made her a prey to those who would love nothing more than to exploit those methods for their own purpose.

After her bedroom door clicked shut, Cassia started tearing the tight braids out of her updo. Within minutes, she was startled by a knock. She opened it at once, not pretending she was at liberty to refuse anyone who the guards let through.

Peter stepped in, sending her slippered feet retreating backward until she plopped into the bed. He took the chair by her looking glass.

"I wanted the chance to talk to you without Radomir hovering behind. I pretended to listen to his ravings and then sent him to bed."

Her hands trembled. "Thank you for being willing to hear me out."

Peter reached his hands out to hold hers. "Tell me how this happened."

She took a deep breath. Aline was perhaps the most painful barrier remaining between them. "The healer who later adopted me. She transferred her abilities to me to save my life."

He lowered his head to rest on their joined hands. "Then why did she not deliver you back to the castle?"

"Perhaps she knew you would not accept a changed woman with powers," she said gently, though her eyebrows raised as she hoped to communicate that that was exactly what had happened.

"I was denied the chance to try." His voice was small.

"You lost me and went down a path of anger and misunderstanding. We can't change the past, but we can try to do better now."

He raised his head, his gaze uncertain. It wasn't the complete transformation she'd hoped for, but he seemed to be listening for once. "I don't know if I can marry a woman I can't fully trust to not one day endanger the kingdom. You've aligned yourself with criminals and proven you can weaken our defenses. Isn't there any way you can get rid of the power?"

Cassia groaned. "You don't understand that this is a part of who I am now. I don't want to get rid of it. I can heal, I can help."

He grimaced. "Can't you just do so using the normal methods?"

"And pretend that I didn't give away the chance to save people? Pretend that the last six years of my life didn't happen? I will not."

"You will not, but you could if you were willing?"

She paused. This piece of information she didn't want to let go of, knowing how Peter had forced his own will on her before. But given enough time and Radomir's calculating, Peter would likely figure it out on his own and trust Cassia less for withholding the truth.

"I could, as Aline did. I could transfer my power to one other, one time, and not die, if they were pure of heart."

"Then that is what you must do." Unbelievable. Had Peter's trauma from losing Alessandra blinded him so fully to the possibilities of what good healing could do? The fact that he ordered Aline's death, that he still resisted Cassia now, revealed the truth.

"Transfer it to who? Will you treat this new vessel with understanding? And who can be trusted with such a gift? Your advisor is trying to manipulate you."

Peter gripped his temples. "Everyone is making me feel like I am weak!"

She grabbed his arm to soften her words. "You are if you refuse to listen to wise counsel to save your own pride. But you don't have to stay that way." She slid her hand back to her lap as she looked into his eyes, hoping to infuse their expression with the same sort of belief that she used to have in him.

For once, her frustration was replaced with compassion. For a long time, no one had been left to believe in him except his younger brother, the next in line to the throne. That must have been lonely.

She could understand the need to hold on too tightly after a great loss. But if Peter was going to exercise his right to remain unyielding to the wrong cause, she could certainly exercise her right to remain unyielding for the right one.

"This gift was entrusted to me because my mother thought I'd be strong enough to make the right decision. I'm not afraid of what will happen to me if you refuse to let me keep it."

"You're the one refusing. Refusing to honor the promises we made. Refusing to see another option. Refusing to lay down your power so that we can be together." His face hardened once again, and he stood. "I've heard enough."

Agonized, Cassia asked, "So nothing is going to happen to Radomir for trying to kill my mother?"

"He was trying to expose you for what you are."

"Are you sure Radomir has no magic, to have bewitched you from hearing any reason?"

"I'm not as foolish as you believe." The set of his face was weary but intent. "I know that Radomir desires power, but he has remained by my side and helped me through the most horrific time of my life. Which is more than I can say of you."

Peter's doggedness sparked Cassia's outrage. "I think the most horrific time of my life was beholding the woman who singlehandedly cared for me for six years, torn to shreds before my eyes. That would have to be the worst. And who caused that to happen? Peter? Radomir? Or is there a difference anymore?"

"I do care for you, Alessandra. But I don't know what to do with you. Is it too dangerous to keep you by my side, to let you roam around stirring up conspiracies with my subjects?"

"I'm not the danger to your throne." She let the statement hang, since he wouldn't hear further accusations about Radomir. If Peter was as capable as he wanted everyone to see him to be, he would investigate further. Maybe she had planted a seed, at least.

"I'll see you tomorrow." Peter stormed out, leaving Cassia once again ignorant of her fate.

13

Though Peter knew Cassia may have been manipulating him just as much as she claimed Radomir was, doubts about his chancellor kept him up until he instructed his chamberlain to arrange a meeting with Radomir in the library before breakfast.

Peter paced back and forth, ignoring the beauty of the illuminated manuscript spines stacked on the shelves and the comfort of his fur-lined seat until Radomir arrived.

"You wanted to see me, Your Highness?"

Peter came straight to the point. "You've been a faithful servant to me, but nothing is the same now that Alessandra arrived. I feel a strong conviction to start over, to clear out my royal staff so that I can be sure I am making my own decisions. You will retain your honored properties, of course."

Radomir crossed his arms. "And retire there, I assume? On the edge of obscurity?"

"I understand this seems a sudden change. But I believe it is what's best for the kingdom." Though his voice sounded firm, Peter's heart beat faster in anticipation of how Radomir might react.

You are the king, not him, Peter chided himself.

Radomir grasped Peter's forearm. "This is exactly what she wants! To strike when you have eliminated your mentors, and you are at your weakest."

Peter shrugged off Radomir's thin, grasping fingers. "This is not a discussion. I have made my decision."

Radomir wheezed, and for a moment Peter considered shouting for a physician. Radomir, who never had one hair out of place, was shaking, and his eyes rolled back in his head. The old man bent over his left hip.

"Are you all right?" Peter stepped closer to steady Radomir and was met by a sharp dagger of steel wedged into his chest. His breath heaved as he collapsed on the ground, knocking over the library's lectern. How had he been so deceived, as to trust this villain for so long?

Radomir sprang upright, laughing manically. "You imbecile. Trying to get rid of me with a few pretty words. At least I am rid of your incompetence at last."

Peter opened his mouth to try and make a sound, but only blood gurgled out.

Cassia awoke with a start. To pain. Injury. A fatal injury, to the heart. She ran to the door and banged her fists on the wood. "Help! The king is in danger, help!"

The knight who opened her door was skeptical. "This better not be one of your tricks. How can you tell that the king's in danger? What did you do?"

"I can feel it as part of my power." They were wasting time Peter didn't have. Cassia shoved past him, and although the knight ran behind her immediately, he did not restrain her.

She could sense the danger more urgently the closer she got to Peter. Aline had told her enough to know that some wounds, there was no coming back from. This was one of those wounds, but it wouldn't stop Cassia from trying.

If only Aline had trained her to strengthen her healing skills! As it was, Cassia only felt comfortable being close to Peter for such a deadly injury. What on earth had happened?

"Let me through." She pulled on the spaulder of the knight guarding the library door in an attempt to yank him away from the entrance, which of course didn't work. "The king is badly injured."

The knight thrust his hand out to stop Cassia, but he opened the door a sliver to find his king suffering on the ground. After he darted in, Cassia and her guard followed.

"Get Prince Cristian," she commanded her guard as she fell on her knees before her former betrothed. It was strange. Glimmers appeared of a time when he kneeled before her prostrate body, begging her to stay with him. Before Aline had granted Cassia the gift which had saved her life.

Radomir tried to run, but the guard who had been stationed outside the library tackled him. "Unhand me. I'm innocent," the arrogant man cried. This time, no one paid him any heed. He'd been found in the middle of mayhem too many times to escape suspicion now.

Cassia put her hands on either side of Peter's wound and in vain tried to send in healing energy. The wound closed and the blood stopped flowing, but it was already too late. Peter was gasping for breath, his eyes growing wide before meeting hers. And there was something else that she sensed. Goodness. Regret. What she had hoped to be within him all along.

"There is a way I can save you," she whispered. "You must become the new healer. Heal now, instead of taking life."

She heard the door reopen and the heavy footfalls of several men, but Cassia kept her eyes on Peter's.

"Don't let your prejudice stand in the way anymore. Will you accept my help?"

His eyes looked desperate for any other option, but already the breath was expiring in his lungs. He closed his eyes and nodded weakly before lowering his head back down to the floor.

Cassia placed her hands gently on Peter's shoulders. "I know it's hard to put so much trust in someone else. I've lost my family twice. Now it feels like I'm losing myself again. I pray to the Maker," the term felt unfamiliar but right as she reached the end of her own ability, "that you will use my gift well and that we both can rise from the ashes."

She thrust her gift into Peter's body, crying out from the effort. Her arms shook and her head lurched back, until his essence was all she could see. The roots of his hair, the pigmentation in his golden skin, bleaching out. It was working.

After a few heart-wrenching moments, Peter's lungs regained their function, this time strong and whole. He gasped and his eyes shot open, his hand reaching for Cassia.

Exhausted though she was, she held him. "It's going to be okay. You'll get through this."

Cristian sunk to his knees beside his brother and placed a hand on his shoulder. "We'll make sure of that."

"You're a good man, Peter," Cassia reiterated. "The Maker would not have entrusted you with such power if you weren't."

Peter looked down at his blanched hand, then focused on Cristian instead. "Where's Radomir?"

"In irons, where he belongs."

Peter nodded.

"Peter?" Cassia asked, saying nothing more until his eyes, now as pale as a frosted windowpane, met her own. "I'm afraid, too. Something is missing that I gave to you. I know you feel broken, but I promise, you are more whole now than you have ever been. Perhaps we can discover our new lives together."

As friends, as allies in a common struggle against the unknown. Cassia now realized they had been thrust together, not to rekindle their romance, but to strengthen each other in this unforeseen time.

"I feel so confused," Peter said in a quieter voice than she had ever heard him use.

"I understand." She nudged his shoulder with her own. "Who knows? The unexpected might be good."

He took a slow breath. "Maybe so."

Cassia followed his lead and breathed the tension away. "It's freeing, you know. Not wrapping every thought into the predetermined image we must bear. When our image has been blasted away, what is left but to discover a new one?"

"Oh, Alessandra. *Cassia.* You always did have a way of making things look bright again. You're shining even more now than you did before, and that gives me great hope."

She gazed up and out the room's one small window. "I think I might know where to begin."

Cassia held Guy's hand on the way to the tree. The parchment map Elaine had found for her turned out to be surprisingly accurate.

Peter did not seem resentful of the couple's close contact. Instead, as Cristian prepared to take over the kingship, the former king seemed content in all things to stand back and listen—to take in and learn as he adjusted to the new life thrust upon him.

His final acts were to free Guy's father, to replace Lord John of Westcombe, and to formally pardon Stephen and Mack's entire family. Mack was tasked with working with the new lord, to make sure that farms would support the crown cooperatively and productively with sufficient resources left over for those who worked the land.

When Cassia heard the soft trickle of water over rocks, she knew they were close.

As they walked, the clear little brook soon transformed into a sparkling, mighty river, full of fat, vibrant, and iridescent fish with long, feathery tails. In the midst of the widest point of the river grew a massive tree with outstretched roots and branches that nearly blocked out the sky.

Its trunk seemed intricately woven together by a master's hand. The leaves were dark, waxy, and thick, and fruits dripped from its branches in flashes of bright orange, butter yellow, rich gold, deep red, emerald, peridot, amethyst, aquamarine, sapphire, coral, cream, and glistening white.

"And the leaves of the tree were for the healing of the nations," Cassia breathed out the line scribbled on the bottom of her mother's map.

Peter fell to his knees, and it was evident he was starting to believe what Cassia had been telling him all along. His difference was not a curse to be eradicated, but a gift to nourish his people for their good.

Even as empty as Cassia now felt, she was learning that they all had a gift to give. One only had to lift their eyes to the Maker to see it.

Ayra's Answer

Chapter One

"I'm sorry, Your Highness. The emperor has concealed the severity of his illness from you for some time." The physician adjusted the wide sleeves of his thick red robe before meeting Ayra's eyes. "He has weeks left to live, and the time has come to prepare the empire." He bowed and left Ayra and Brome standing outside her father's chamber door.

Ayra whirled on Brome. "Did you know?"

"I... suspected as much." His posture was repentant.

Ayra kept her face controlled, but felt an internal pang that, once again, her father had seen fit to include the conniving head of Lancily's military in his plans, but not his own daughter. Not the one whose life would now be completely uprooted.

She rapped on his dark pine door. A servant answered and stepped back to admit them both into the lavish receiving hall which led into the emperor's bedroom.

The emperor's personal attendant opened the entry to Kang's room, where Ayra's father was predictably seated at his writing desk instead of resting as he should. He stood, though the movement caused his face to flicker with pain. "The physician spoke to you, then. Good. Now, to make arrangements."

Ayra straightened her posture as was expected of her, but subtly ran her fingertips over the pink stitching on her skirt to steady herself. "Arrangements regarding the law of succession."

"Precisely. You must choose a groom of royal blood to guide you before you take control of the empire. However, our nearest neighbor has lately engaged himself in a love match with his courtier." Kang's face twisted with distaste at the thoughtlessness of this choice. "So, I've gained the approval of the council to amend our law."

Ayra clasped her hands in thanks. "Father, your trust in me means so much. I won't let you down."

Kang extended his hand to silence her. "The council has agreed to amend our law so that your choice of husband may be a trusted ruler of our own state."

Ayra gasped, regarding Brome. She was sure the council was greatly in favor of the suggestion to elevate one among their own ranks.

Brome was always perfectly put-together in a way that made her stomach churn with distrust. He never told Kang anything other than exactly what he wanted to hear, but where her father saw dutiful obedience, Ayra sensed a cloying ambition that had propelled Brome precisely to this moment.

"Does not the king of Lynebrook have an unmarried older brother?" Ayra burst out, knowing any pleas to rule alone would only incite her father's anger.

Lynebrook had been a contentious bordering state as of late, but perhaps the disgraced Prince Peter would allow her to rule her people and be content to reign as an honorable figurehead. She'd take the unknown over an unsettling usurper like Brome.

"You finally wish to respect the ceremonial law?" Kang regarded her, eyebrows raised. "At the sunset of my life, perhaps my words have at last taken effect. Very well. I will arrange a meeting with Prince Peter of Lynebrook. If he doesn't meet with our approval, then Brome will be waiting to perform his duty to his country."

Brome nodded solemnly, causing the tassels on his wide-brimmed hat to sway. "Shall I go to Lynebrook now, to ensure the safe delivery of this important message?"

Kang gestured towards the door. "Make haste. My days are few, and I would have this matter settled before I'm gone."

He sat back down at his desk, as if to dismiss them both. Brome swiftly departed, but Ayra lingered. "I am sorry to hear about your declining health," she said.

He picked up his pen and began writing. "We all must die sometime. I'm only sorry my time has come when there has been upheaval between our kingdoms." He ceased from his work to look at her. "You should consider Brome. He would be a strong leader."

Ayra was careful to keep her nod submissive. "I love our people. I have studied for my entire life to take on this work."

"Love is not enough. Studies are not enough. The lower classes will revolt if they sense any weakness during a change of power."

Ayra pursed her lips. "Or, they may appreciate that I have been among them all these years."

"Doing charity work. Making public appearances." Kang stroked his thin mustache. "That is much different than commanding an army."

"I will take good counsel."

"Then take this. Marry well. Secure our common prosperity." He loosened the neck of his tunic.

Was he fevering now? Ayra wished to rush toward her father, to call the physician back to minister to him. But she simply said, "I promise to do so." If only he could see how their common prosperity was all she had worked for. All she wanted.

"May the Maker give you strength." Kang returned to his work.

Ayra bowed her head. His send-off phrase was customary for their people. Lancily loved their ceremonies and celebrations, but few truly believed in the power of a Maker anymore. Still, Ayra repeated prayer to herself as she walked away. "May the Maker give me strength."

Her steps echoed loudly through the curving corridors, and the sound made her feel more alone. She would need to be crafty to outwit a foreign prince, a slippery general, and a single-minded emperor.

Brome saddled Midnight with provisions for the half-day's ride, and soon reached Lynebrook's front gate. He thrust his imperial ring before the guard at the entrance, and received swift escort into the castle after a stable boy relieved him of his horse.

To the young knight who was navigating him through the halls, Brome asked, "How's the new king settling in?"

The boy walked taller. "Oh, wonderfully. We're used to him after so many years at his brother's side, and he has always been popular with the people."

"I see." Meaning the elder brother had not been popular. This could be used to Brome's advantage. "And did the king retain the same chancellor as his brother had, or did he replace the old officials?"

The knight guffawed. The green fool seemed thrilled to share all his kingdom's news. "You haven't heard? Chancellor Radomir tried to assassinate Prince Peter, so King Cristian naturally had him thrown in the dungeon."

Brome was silent for a breath. "You mean to say he's still here? They didn't execute him?"

The knight shook his head and lowered his voice for greater effect. "He's rotting in the dungeon below our very feet."

"Edward, what are you yammering about?" An older guard outside a massive set of wooden doors raised an eyebrow as they approached.

Edward straightened. "Just getting this emissary from Lancily up to speed, Sir Andrew. He comes with an important message for the king."

"Very well. Go back to your post." Sir Andrew accompanied Brome through a library to a large desk with carvings of sycamore leaves on its borders.

The king was a youth with tawny locks and freckles dotting rosy cheeks. Cristian smiled broadly. *This one shouldn't be difficult to extract more information from.*

Brome replicated Cristian's welcoming expression. "I hear congratulations are in order."

Cristian stood to shake his hand. "Thank you, sir. I am exceedingly blessed to be marrying Lady Laurel, the love of my life."

Brome slackened his smile. "And I'm afraid that is why I'm here. Are you familiar with our marriage customs in Lancily?"

Cristian's open demeanor fled from him like a thief in the night. "I recall one interesting detail from my schooling. A female heir must marry a man of royal blood to assume the throne, but surely this time has not come for the emperor's daughter?"

Brome stepped forward conspiratorially, though there was no one else in the room to overhear. "It has. Emperor Kang does not wish to publicize the fact, but he is not in good health."

Cristian's brow furrowed. "You all have my sympathies. But surely you realize I cannot break my engagement."

"Of course not. It has been suggested that your brother may fulfill the requirement." Cristian began to protest, but Brome dug further in.

"He is of upstanding moral character, I hope? We would want the princess to be equally yoked."

Cristian cleared his throat and said, "Of course he is!"

However, his young knight's blathering had told Brome otherwise.

Cristian continued, "I am sure that the princess's amiable qualities surpass even her beauty. I am simply not sure if Peter is ready to be married at this time." The king was trying to be diplomatic, but was starting to sweat.

If Brome had truly been committed to the aim of securing Peter's consent, he may have brought up the fool's recent aggressions against their country to pressure Cristian into an agreement. But he had already displayed an appropriate level of commitment to his emperor's cause.

Instead, he said, "This is a decision that would change the course of his future. It is understandable that the prince would have hesitations. Please send us word as soon as you can. A contingency plan has been developed in case he is unwilling to court the princess."

Cristian knocked his fist on the top of his desk. "Oh, that's a relief. I'll talk with my brother, but I am sure what his answer will be."

"I will take my leave, then."

"Thank you for your message. Please, let my servants know if you have need of a warm meal or any kind of refreshment before returning home."

On the way out of the library, Brome informed Sir Andrew that he could find his way to the exit of the castle on his own. The guard didn't contradict him, but looked too wary for Brome's liking. He would have to be careful not to be followed on his journey.

He *would* find his way out in time. After first finding his way to the dungeon, to talk with this Radomir about whatever secrets this family may hold, should they be foolish enough to accept Kang's offer.

# # #

Cristian looked as if he wanted to grab Peter by the neck and pin him down, but ever making the correct choices, he refrained. "You can't tell me you are considering marrying a near stranger when a month ago you were trying to take over their land."

Peter had enjoyed the recent cessations of his brother's lectures. He sighed deeply to prepare himself for this next one. "That's exactly why

I must consider this alliance. I have done much to damage the relationship between our two nations."

"So, go on a diplomatic mission. Don't secure an engagement. Marriage is not to be taken lightly."

"Not everyone can marry their childhood sweetheart." Peter's words held a bitter edge, though he knew that the sorry way his life had turned out, as compared to his brother's, was Peter's own fault. "Not everything goes according to plan. What else do I have to contribute to this kingdom anymore? I am humiliated."

Cristian's incredulity softened. "Give it time, Peter. Our people know you have been through much, first with Mother and Father dying, then with losing your fiancé..."

"And then I put our people through more. There is no future for me here anymore." Peter stared down at his ivory skin, wondering if anyone had warned the crown princess about his...infirmity.

"Then, your plan is to run away from the problem you created?"

Why couldn't Cristian see the brilliance of this opportunity? "A political agreement may be a way I can fix it."

"And sacrifice yourself in the process?"

Peter shrugged. There were some who believed that he should be in a cell next to Radomir for all his years of neglect and aggression, as much as Cassia and Cristian had tried to talk him into making a fresh start. A marriage to a young princess would be preferrable to the harsher punishment he'd avoided.

He remembered Ayra from when his parents used to host state dinners. She was a pretty young girl, refined, though a little reserved. He did not expect to have a marriage in the traditional sense, but maybe he could offer her the few lessons he'd learned during his ill-fated reign as she fulfilled the requirements of her ceremonial law. Perhaps she would prefer a wedding to him than losing her position. There was only one way to find out.

"I've made up my mind. Will you forbid me, little brother?"

The exasperated tilt to Cristian's chin indicated that he considered using his dictatorial power, as Peter had done countless times during his own reign. But he merely said, "So be it."

Chapter Two

A touch more flattery, a handful of well-placed coins, and not only did young Edward show Brome the way to the dungeon, but he went ahead of him to relieve the knight patrolling Radomir's cell.

The boy was visibly nervous, as he should have been for allowing Brome to pay their enemy a visit. "I'll be at the top of the steps. Please make your conversation quick."

"Of course."

Brome powered through the pungent odor of urine and sweat to meet the man with matted silver hair, seated on the floor with his elbows resting on his knees, counting the stones on the walls as if that were the most diverting task that existed (and for him, it probably was).

Radomir flinched when he first heard his visitor approach. Then, his teeth glinted in an unappealing, dirt-speckled grin.

"What do we have here? An emissary from Lancily. Brome, isn't it? Forgive me for sitting. I'm afraid that nowadays my courtly manners leave much to be desired."

Brome thought it odd that Radomir could speak so flippantly in his present situation. Then again, he supposed the man had nothing left to lose. Brome was banking on that. "I came to see if you'd have information about the former king, Peter. Information that would be interesting to his potential father-in-law."

Radomir wheezed a laugh. "So, Kang is trying to arrange a marriage with Peter. A rather unlikely turn of events. Yes, you could say Peter has a talent that would be of great interest to the emperor."

Brome waved his hand in the air. "I've heard of his skill in swordplay. This matters little to us."

Radomir shuffled forward, and Brome held his breath. "What about...healing people miraculously? As if he had the touch of the Maker himself?"

"The Maker is a load of superstitious nonsense. You're wasting my time." Brome turned to leave.

He heard Radomir leap to his feet. "But I've seen the power at play. His knights are quick to dismiss me, but you seem like a man who would rather know all the possibilities."

Brome turned back. "It does seem odd that Peter stepped down so suddenly. Some even report that his physical appearance has been affected."

"Affected... or bleached two shades lighter and completely transformed..."

Brome pursed his lips. "And this supposed change came from where?"

"His former betrothed, who deposited her gift to him to return to her hovel of poverty."

A sharp cough resounded down the stairs. Edward's warning. "Thank you for the information."

Radomir clutched the bars with his long fingers. "Getting me out of here would be a better thanks."

"Time will tell if the information you've given me is useful. There could be great riches in store for you if Peter falls." Brome took the stairs two at a time, ruminating on the strange tale of the ruined old man.

# # #

Ayra had hoped Peter would answer her summons, but she was surprised when their scouts announced he would be there by the afternoon. Brome had returned already, and had made himself scarce, which Ayra preferred to his attempts to pretend as if he enjoyed her company, rather than simply coveting her crown.

Ayra dressed in her finest embroidered satin, and had her attendant loop her black braid high upon her head into an intricate design, complete with fragrant lilies. She flushed her lips and cheeks with ruby powder, and rubbed orange peels over her wrists.

These were business decisions, rather than for her own enjoyment. She remembered how Peter had stared only at his betrothed on the few functions they'd both been invited to, but any edge Ayra could give herself to sway him to her side, she would use.

After her beautification was complete, she joined her father in the throne room. Of course she would not be allowed to meet her future husband alone and decide for herself what to do. She only hoped Peter would make a good impression, and that her father's love of tradition would overpower his affinity for Brome.

They sat in their respective chairs, her father feigning strength and health by stretching every bit of his spine and fortifying his elbows on the armrest, though she could see beads of sweat darken the gray hair at his temples.

The porters swung the double doors wide, revealing Peter. He carried the same dashing appearance and powerful physique that Ayra had remembered from his teenage years, though the confidence no longer reached his eyes. A robe and crown graced his pale gold features, despite his recent disgrace. She hadn't remembered his hair looking quite that light. Had his kingship aged him so much?

He bowed lowly at the steps under their feet. "I am honored for this invitation."

Ayra tipped her chin. "Thank you for honoring us with your presence. Please, take a seat." She gestured to a plain chair they'd stationed beside her on the wide main platform. Brome, regrettably, sat on the king's other side, almost as if the king was playing matchmaker instead of greeting an important delegate from a neighboring country. Then again, Ayra supposed, a matchmaker Kang would be today. Would he choose the slinking serpent, or the unknown prince? Only the Maker knew.

# # #

Peter's gift scanned the room automatically. All was normal with the servant who admitted him in. Minister Brome's heart was racing, though from normal vision the man betrayed no signs of tension. Every muscle in Ayra's body was stretched to the breaking point, like she carried the wait of her whole country on her petite shoulders. And Emperor Kang—Peter's eyes widened momentarily before he controlled his expression—Kang was slowly dying. Had that been why they'd hastily requested a marriage?

The healing spirit inside of Peter longed to make the emperor whole right then, but caution held him back. He would be suspected if he arrived and the emperor was instantly free from all disease. Let them think that one night of rest and a blessing from the Maker caused Kang to recover. Still, after sensing the princess's heavy breaths, almost to the point of hyperventilation, Peter longed to end Kang's suffering with a thought. A wave of exhaustion crashed over him.

"Father?" Ayra breathed.

Kang stood suddenly, face contorted in disbelief. Had Peter healed him by accident? He still wasn't fully acquainted with the force of his ability.

Cassia had tried to explain all she had learned, but she had abandoned the palace for the small town she once lived in. And now, Peter was alone and endangered in a foreign land.

Brome pointed his finger at Peter. "Witchery!" he cried.

"Your Majesty, you are healed! Surely there is no dark magic afoot," Ayra protested. But Kang was already regarding Peter with intense suspicion. So, Peter did the only thing he could think of now that all of his hopes were spoiled. Run.

Chapter Three

Ayra watched, openmouthed, as Peter shoved past the guards who laid chase outside the throne room. "Father!"

His rebuke was sharp. "You will address me as Your Majesty in public." Ayra shrunk back. She always forgot herself in times of great bewilderment, which, regrettably, fell upon her often. His Majesty steepled his hands. "At least we know now who you should marry."

"I need marry no one now. You are healed."

"Just for once, child, can you do as you're told without argument?"

Ayra didn't mean to deepen the lines on Kang's forehead. But she had to answer back. "And for once, can you listen to what I think?"

Kang turned to Brome. "What have I done to deserve such a disobedient daughter? Have I been lax? Dishonest?"

"No, Emperor."

Hot tears of rage plucked the back of Ayra's eyes. "Why will you listen to him and not to me? It isn't fair." She knew that her father would see her outburst as childish and unacceptable, but she was reaching her breaking point.

Perhaps he could sense as much. "It's been a long day. Go retire to your room."

Maybe she acted like a child because she was always treated as such. Well, no more. No more waiting to see if her father would ever change. No more sacrifices "for the good of the country." She knew now that not even a near-death experience could make her father wake up to who were his friends and who were his enemies.

She ran out of the room, but not to her chambers. She ran out the front door, and straight past the gate.

# # #

Peter had forsaken his mount, and the mighty former king had instead scaled a tree like a ruffian to avoid Lancily's patrols sent to lay chase. He settled on a sturdy limb above the lattice of leaves below him when he saw Ayra in her beautiful gown, stumbling down the road with tears streaming down her face.

Chivalry outweighed personal preservation, and he slid his fingers down the rough bark to hang from the lowest branch. She shrieked.

"What are you doing out here?" Peter asked.

"What just happened wasn't right. The kingdom hasn't been run correctly in a long time, and I'm sorry I dragged you into this marriage plot." Ayra continued her run then, and Peter dropped down to follow after.

"You didn't drag me into anything. Do you often take responsibility for other people's problems?"

Ayra looked as if he'd given her a steady splash from a stream. "I don't know. I would like to break free from that habit, but I have to break free from these grounds first."

"That makes two of us."

Ayra's delicate eyebrows shot upward. "Can't you go back to your brother?"

"I came here to get away from Lynebrook. I embroiled it in scandal which will only grow greater after this morning's events." Peter panted from the exertion of their flight, so soon after healing Kang. The futility of their situation didn't help his energy, either. It seemed that every time he tried to direct his life on a new course, his efforts veered sideways.

"Is it true, then? Did you heal my father?" she asked, her soulful brown eyes wide.

"I did. Didn't mean to on the spot, but there is an instinct within me now to heal so strongly that I couldn't help it, feeling your pain so close." He shook his head. "The emperor's pain, rather."

"Is this instinct why your coloring has lightened?"

"Yes. Healing power was the last thing I would have asked for. But you can say the Maker had different plans for me."

"I think I know what you mean." Ayra gestured that they should start walking through the trees—to where, he didn't know. "My inquisitive spirit has always vexed my father. I've always felt out of place. You believe in a Maker. Why do you think He made us become this way if it makes our lives more difficult?"

"Perhaps there is a purpose at work we haven't yet seen. I certainly hope so."

A Lancily soldier stepped out from behind a tree and Peter moved to shield Ayra, but the slender man put his hands out. "Please, I mean no harm. It's only that I overheard your conversation, and I feel the same way."

Ayra looked at him in puzzlement. "Jun?"

"Yes, Your Highness. I have powers, like this man. I can see things before they happen. I've been too afraid to tell until now. But there is at least one other like us. Let me take you to her."

"Jun, you've served our empire faithfully for years. How do I know you aren't lying, to lead us back to my father?"

"I'm not lying, but where else do you have to go? Another patrol will come by in twelve minutes. If you don't believe me, you'll be found." Jun hurried back into the forest.

Ayra looked to Peter, who shrugged. They followed the enigmatic soldier through the forest until they came to a little farm. Laboring over a row of small sprouts was a peasant woman, her hair tied up in a rag. Upon seeing Ayra, the woman tore off her work gloves and bowed.

"Please, be at ease." Ayra touched her shoulder.

"Your Highness, my name is Hayen. Welcome to my home. Had I but known you were coming..."

"A place to sit will be more than sufficient, Hayen."

Hayen dipped her head, her eyes still downcast, and hurried to admit them through her front door.

She only had two wooden stools around her rough-hewn table, but Jun plopped down on the dirt floor, and Peter followed suit.

"Hayen, I've learned that the princess and this man—Prince Peter of Lynebrook?" Jun gave him a questioning look, and Peter nodded, "— may have an ability like ours. In truth, an ability much stronger than ours." At Jun's words, Hayen inhaled sharply.

"Hayen, you have nothing to fear," Ayra repeated. "What is your ability?"

"My voice," she whispered.

"Pardon?" Peter said. He found it hard to believe a slight girl who could hardly project her words across the room would be gifted in voice.

"Show them." Jun put a gentle hand on Hayen's shoulder.

"My voice," Hayen repeated, meeting Peter's eyes. Peter ducked his head and covered his ears. It was if he had heard her voice from inside his mind, reverberating like a gong struck by a strongman.

"I can make people hear me in any language I choose." She turned to Ayra and quipped a phrase in the rapid court dialect of Lancily, which Peter had woefully neglected in his childhood studies.

Ayra's eyes widened. "She spoke perfectly."

Jun ran his fingers through his close-cropped hair. "We think the gifts originate from a stream, deep in the forest. I stumbled upon it once during a scouting patrol. It was the sweetest, coolest water I've ever tasted. Strange visions came upon me after I drank, so I was scared to tell a soul until Hayen fell sick."

He looked on her with affection. "My instinct was correct. She drank and she was healed, but never the same. It's like the water enhances something deep inside us that we were born with."

"Visions?" Peter asked skeptically. Jun's description of a river matched the one by the mystical tree which Cassia had shown him, and at this point, Peter could believe nearly anything, but still, each layer pulled back to reveal a new world was disorienting.

Jun laughed. "My brother always claimed I had a sixth sense, about when harsh weather would come, or what a person would decide to do. But intuition grew to something much more." His face grew serious. "I wish I could go back to before the gift. I have seen things I wish I could forget. I cannot always share my visions, in the fear that I'll destroy the future. But I saw the two of you in the forest. That's how I knew where to look for you."

Ayra clutched Jun's arm. "You must tell me. Will my father forgive me? What will happen to the kingdom?"

Jun's wide-set eyes went glassy. "You will have to go back and face what you left. If you do not, your father will die."

Ayra turned her desperate gaze toward Peter. "His illness will return?"

Jun shook himself back to full consciousness. Pity and pain splashed across his features. "His minister seeks to kill him as we speak. The emperor will name him as successor, and the fiend will repay him with murder."

"Then I must go to him," Ayra cried.

"But will he hear you?" Peter asked softly.

Ayra gestured toward Jun, asking for more prophecy, but Jun shook his head. "This is the problem. I cannot see everything. Only short glimpses that could be misinterpreted. I'm sorry."

Ayra sniffed and straightened on her hard seat. "Thank you for what you've already shared."

"Is there anything that would convince your father of Brome's guilt?" Peter asked.

"Only if the evidence was indisputable, right before his eyes. His preference runs that deep."

"And Brome doesn't strike me as someone who would act so carelessly."

"Then, we make our way back to the palace. Wait for Brome to make his move." At Ayra's words, Peter was struck by the difference between them.

He had first slunk away from his kingdom when Kang proposed the marriage, and second, fled away like a vagabond as soon as Brome exposed his powers.

Ayra had spoken, not of usurping her father's place, or preserving her own life, but of saving the father who, first, had attempted to marry her off to the likes of Peter, and second, disregarded all her concerns in the throne room. Such single-minded love was rare indeed.

"This sounds dangerous." Jun pulled at the loose threads at his tunic's hem.

"You don't have to get involved. But this sounds like my only option." Ayra crossed her regal arms, and the matter was settled. The tragic irony of her succession battle was that Ayra was a natural-born leader. Peter, Jun, and Hayen would all follow to protect her.

Chapter Four

The four new allies ate and slept on woven blankets on Hayen's floor.
Once the morning sun burned, they set off for Emperor Kang's colorful
stone stronghold. They watched from a distance as guards prowled
around the palace's perimeter, under the shelter of its shining rooftop
tiles.

"Now what?" Ayra asked.

"We have to get in there and witness what is going on."

"Impossible," Ayra said. "Even in the dead of night, the palace is
closely supervised."

"Could we disguise ourselves?"

"Hardly." Ayra pushed Peter's broad shoulder with one finger, and
then, a lovely blush colored her cheeks.

Jun cleared his throat. Peter had forgotten that Jun and Hayen were
there. "Your power is healing, yes?" Jun asked.

"Yes."

"How far can you heal from?"

"I've never tried to heal from a distance, but if I concentrate now, I
can sense the people inside the castle."

"Can you tell which person is which?"

"With some effort, I believe I can." Peter closed his eyes. His
consciousness zipped from stranger to stranger until honing in on
Emperor Kang in his chambers, and Brome consulting with some
other men in a secluded study. He shuddered and reopened his eyes.

"You were able to sense the emperor?"

"I was. Immediately I received a sense of health. I think, if he was still ill, I would be able to heal him."

Jun's expression was grim. "What about if he was poisoned?"

"You're not saying I wait for Brome to poison him, and then heal him from out here?"

Jun tapped his chin. "It would be a risk, but success is one possible future."

"And what's the other possible future?" Ayra asked.

Jun's brow furrowed. "We'll have to work together to ensure you're not disturbed."

"That's comforting," Peter deadpanned. "How long do we have?"

"Roughly a day. The assassination attempt will happen tomorrow. We need to get you comfortable, and after that it wouldn't hurt to monitor Kang frequently. We want to be sure my timing is right." Jun strapped on his curved blade and left for his morning duty.

They'd agreed that the fewer interruptions to normal operations of the palace, the safer they would be. Jun had even promised to lead any search parties away from their hiding place.

That night, Hayen and Ayra surrounded Peter as he slept. They dared not even build a fire. Peter woke with hunger pangs and ate a few handfuls of hawthorn berries they had plucked from some nearby bushes.

How he longed for a plate of salty, roasted pork. He would even take a fat pheasant. But, no, he had to focus. Brome could be poisoning Kang's wine any moment now, just as Radomir once had done to Cassia's mother.

Peter didn't like to think of Cassia. The woman who was once his fiancé had chosen someone else. But her memory didn't sting as much as it did a few weeks ago. He was staying busy now. He was meeting new people, including a selfless young woman with silky dark hair and intelligent eyes.

Peter shook his head clear and scanned for Kang. He only used his power to reach out every few minutes, as it tired him, and he did not want to run out of energy before having to heal the emperor.

He would have to let Kang feel the effects of the sickness for a moment so that he would believe their testimony, but not so long that Peter's power could not reach him anymore. Jun's foggy predictions did little to ease Peter's nerves.

The next time Peter scanned, Kang was choking, taking thick heaving breaths. Peter tried to hold the urge to heal back, temporarily breaking his concentration to study his physical surroundings. Kang couldn't think he was choking on his morning breakfast.

A few more wheezes and Peter's healing power lashed out in the direction of the palace, forcing the poison which was slowly sleeping into Kang's bloodstream to slink backwards.

Peter swooned from fatigue, and the last thing he remembered was Ayra's arms breaking his fall as he dropped to the ground.

# # #

Peter had told Ayra that he may pass out from the effort of healing her father, but she couldn't breathe until the color returned to his face, and his eyes fluttered open. She greeted him with a suffocating hug before self-consciously sitting back on her heels. "Thank you. Thank you for healing my father. Thank you for everything you've done."

"Any decent fellow would have done the same," Peter said, massaging his clammy hands.

"The rumors are already flying out to the countryside from the palace servants," Hayen said. "The emperor has made a wonderous recovery from an attempt on his life."

Peter nodded, shaking out his tingling limbs. "It's time, then."

"He still may not believe me," Ayra warned. Most likely not. "But I'm done with never speaking out in fear of being rejected." Her heart still fluttered at the thought of her father's anger, but she could live more easily with the discomfort than she could the shame of staying silent.

"If your father does not see you as a blessing, that is his blindness and his loss." His assurance caused Ayra's clenched fists to loosen. "You can come to Lynebrook if I'm welcomed back after all of this."

"Let's pray you can return to Lynebrook a hero, accepted and vindicated after today is done." Maybe she could go to Lynebrook, if her father turned her away.

Ayra swallowed. *Maker, help us. If you're real, we can't do this alone.* She listened, but heard no answer. She turned to the diminutive girl beside them. "Hayen, are you sure you want to come with us?"

"A life in hiding is no life at all. It's time for all of us to be honest, and to give hope for others like us," Hayen answered, her quiet voice brimming with eloquence.

"Let's do it then." Ayra set her face like the brave princess she always had to be, this time not feeling like it was a facade. Playing it safe had done her no favors in the past. She would accept whatever was next for her, and let go of the vision of serving Lancily from the throne if her father would not allow her to fulfill her deepest wish.

As soon as they stepped onto the clay path on the way to the palace, guards spotted them and yelled, "It's the princess and Prince Peter!"

The three of them were seized and escorted to an immediate audience with the emperor. And, of course, with his Minister of War.

Kang sat, formidable, upon his throne. "My absconding daughter." It was not the welcome Ayra had hoped for, but was that relief on his face?

She lifted her chin. "How could I stay here, when sense and rule of law has fled Lancily? Father, you are alive because of Peter! He could have run away, but he helped me instead and saved you a second time."

Kang stroked his beard. "So, these strange happenings were due to Peter again?" He stabbed his finger in Peter's direction. "How do I know that you didn't have me poisoned, just to earn my forgiveness?"

"Forgiveness?" Ayra kneaded her forehead with her fingertips, attempting to remain calm. "He's done nothing but help you!"

"Through what power?" Kang leaned closer.

Peter answered, "I believe the Maker has granted a great gift to me, an unworthy recipient, perhaps to display that it is His own merit at work and not my own."

"These are wise words. Yet, who poisoned me?"

"A man from your own court, I am afraid to say. Your Majesty, the mastermind behind this plot is your minister of war."

"Brome?"

Brome strode forward. "Believe nothing this deceiver says."

Peter ignored him. "Did you not recently name Brome your successor?"

A rare display of hurt displayed across the emperor's face. Ayra's father was not too far gone after all.

All of the times Ayra had warned him before must have clicked together with the events of the past few days to create a picture too obvious to ignore.

"Who is this usurper, anyway?" Brome threw his hand in Hayen's direction.

"Your Majesty, we are your humble citizens, and are also gifted." Jun took a hesitant step forward from a line of soldiers.

Hayen amplified her voice for all to hear in their mind, and Kang flinched like a swarm of bees had come upon him. His guards rushed to his side, but Kang waved them away.

She said, "Please grant us our freedom to live in peace. I did not choose for my gift to manifest in this way, but I do not wish to remain quiet anymore."

"A gift? From where?" Kang demanded.

Hayen removed her balled-up fists from her simple dress, soiled from their time outdoors. "I once drunk from a stream of life which made me stronger than I ever thought possible. Perhaps you too can visit this enchanted hollow, and gain a gift that could make you an even more skilled ruler. I just ask that you see us as we are, loyal subjects, servants with a heart to give, and keep an open mind."

Kang lowered his head back to rest at the top of his bright, lacquered throne. "This is much to comprehend."

Ayra leapt up the few steps separating her from her father and took his hand. "I'd like to comprehend it with you, if you'll allow me."

"We all would," Peter added.

"Send Brome to the dungeon, until he is investigated," Kang commanded. Panic broke forth on Brome's expression, but Ayra couldn't bring herself to feel pity for him. He had pushed, sabotaged, and manipulated his way to the position that he truly deserved.

Ayra turned to Peter, her triumphant smile dimmed a bit at the idea of him leaving. "I suppose you will return home and settle matters with your family."

"Yes. But I would like to come back to call, with your permission."

Ayra nodded eagerly.

"And the emperor's?"

Kang lifted his hands, suddenly jovial. "You are of royal blood, after all!"

Peter lifted his chin to the heavens, and Hayen put the emotions he was displaying in his physical form into lovely, spiritual words.

"May the Maker be praised for His beautiful plan. Who foresaw a second chance for this man. The gift he had hated, turned into gold, to save his love's love, now the future unfolds."

THE END

Acknowledgments

All glory to God, who put a piece of this story in my heart in middle school and helped me through all of its challenges. Thank you for healing me through the power of Your words, and for showing me that being with You, in whatever place You would wish me to be, is enough.

Thank you to Savanna for your life-saving suggestions, Tori, Sofie, Belen, Dad, and Mom for early reading and support, and all who offered encouragement through this process!

To my family, who gives me reasons to write and live with gladness.

From my local library, I enjoyed reading the research compiled in *Arms and Armor of the Medieval Knight* by David Edge and John Miles Paddock, and *Everyday Life in Medieval Times* by Marjorie Rowling. Though my book is fantasy and not historical fiction, I tried to give it a medieval feel! Any inaccuracies are my own.

Thank you, reader, for picking up my story. Independent authors rely on your reviews and sharing with friends and family. I pray that this novella encourages you to embrace your spiritual gifts and further God's kingdom. Blessings!

About the Author

Rachel Blanchard is a teacher, wife, and mother of three young children. She loves frequenting theme parks and bookstores in sunny Central Florida! She is passionate about sharing lessons learned, and the message that we can trust in God's goodness.

Also Available from Rachel Blanchard

Small-Town Romances
First in My Heart
Finding My Heart